RESTORATION IN THE BARRENS

A novel by Joe Riederer

Big Bluestem Press

ISBN: 0-9671386-0-4

Library of Congress Number: 99-62229

Big Bluestem Press
12321 87th Street South
Wisconsin Rapids, Wisconsin 54494

Printed in the United States of America by
Palmer Publications, Inc.
Layout and design by Amherst Press

Cover photo by Bob Bergstrom

For Mom and Dad

Acknowledgements

The author would like to thank Lynn DuPree, Fran Hamerstrom, Jim Riederer, Rob Nurre, Gib Endrizzi, Chris Roerden, Eric Lobner, and Mat Pankratz for their many hours of editing and proofreading.

1

Madison, Wisconsin

"Okay Corey, this is your last chance." The woman pulled on her winter parka. "Are you sure you don't want to come with Dad and me?"

The boy looked up from the living room floor, set down the *National Wildlife Magazine*, and smiled. "I don't know how to break it to you Mom, but that movie sounds pretty boring to me."

"Me too!" came a voice from down the hall. "But you don't see me trying to get out of it, do you?"

"Sorry, Dad, you lost the race—you're stuck."

"I was set up. That race wasn't fair!"

The woman handed a parka to the man and grinned. "Face it, you lost. I ski better than you and you know it!"

The man rolled his eyes and groaned. The two adults walked out into the January night. A ghost of wintry air crawled into the small apartment as the door closed. With his parents gone for the night, the young boy returned to his magazine. He grabbed one of the homemade afghans his mother had strategically placed around the living room and wrapped it around him to ward off the cold. Within minutes, he was asleep.

The doorbell rang. Only half awake, the boy opened the door. In the cold entryway stood a City of Madison police officer and a woman from the Dane County Child Welfare Department. This was when Corey's world fell apart.

2
The Meeting

The child in the passenger seat had not said a word during the ninety-seven mile trip north from Madison. Every attempt at conversation produced nothing more than brief grunts that could not be mistaken for words. Only two times did the boy seem to react in any way: once, when a red-tailed hawk passed low over the car; and again when, forgetting she wasn't alone, Cindy Dalea began singing along to *American Pie* as she drove.

Cindy didn't know much about this boy. Coming back from the first real vacation she'd had in years, she had not had enough time to look over the case file. What did she know about this kid? He was thirteen, a little on the skinny side, and had sandy brown hair that fell into his eyes. His mother and father had been killed when a drunk teenager driving her parents' car had hit their car. For the last three months, the boy had been passed around from one relative to the next. He had never been in trouble with the law and, until the accident, seemed to like school. It was slightly unusual to place a child so far away from home; but there were a few foster openings in Adams County, while Dane County was bursting at the seams.

In the nineteen years that Cindy had been working for the Adams County Social Services Department, she'd had this responsibility too many times. Introducing a foster child to foster parents was emotionally taxing. The child knows he is here because he is not safe, or not wanted, anywhere else. He also knows that his foster parents are being paid to take him in. Most important, he knows he's here for only a short time.

Cindy winced as her blue 1991 Chevy Suburban scraped the large snow bank that bordered the driveway. The farmhouse needed paint badly. The sidewalk to the house was shoveled neatly, but the path to the barn still showed the results of yesterday's heavy snow. Behind the barn lay a one-hundred-sixty-acre potato field with a large center-pivot irrigation boom that stretched to the western fence line. The snow-covered field looked lifeless. Cindy had an uneasy feeling as she brought the large Chevy to a stop.

Ellen and Ben Raine came out of the house immediately. "A good sign," Cindy thought. She had never met the Raines. This was their first foster child. The report in the file explained that until 1988 they had been struggling dairy farmers. The worst drought in fifty years and some heartbreaking financial trouble led to their selling off most of the farm. Ben started driving for a local trucking firm and sometimes was gone for days at time. Ellen did seasonal work packing cheese gift boxes and taking telephone orders for a company in Marshfield.

Ellen, Ben, and Cindy stood in the farmyard talking as the boy slowly got out of the car. The adults stopped talking and Cindy moved to stand next to the anxious child. "Corey Nelson, I'd like you to meet Mr. and Mrs. Raine," Cindy said.

"Please, call us Ben and Ellen," Ben said, offering his hand.

Corey shook it hesitantly. "Nice to meet you," Corey said, a slight nervous quiver to his voice. "Thank you for letting me stay here."

Ellen stepped forward and shook Corey's hand. "We're glad you're here. Let's all go inside. It's cold out here. Ms. Dalea, would you like some coffee?"

"Please call me 'Cindy,' and, yes, I would love a cup." The conversation seemed forced as the group took seats around the circular kitchen table. "Corey, would you like a cup of hot chocolate?" Ellen offered.

"No thank you," came the automatic reply.

"Cindy tells us that you're quite the outdoorsman. Do you hunt much?" Ben asked.

"No. We…" He caught himself. "I mean, I don't hunt. I just like to be out-doors."

"You're in luck. Just down the road is the Mary G. Lincoln Wildlife Area. The locals just call it 'the Barrens.' It covers over fifteen square miles," Ben added. Corey's interest was heightened, if for only a few seconds.

"I know this must be overwhelming to you," Ellen said calmly. "How about if we take you up to your room and give you a chance to unpack. We'll take some time to talk later."

Cindy saw this as her cue to leave. "Ellen, I'll talk with you tomorrow to see how things are going. Feel free to call me at home if you have any questions." With that she finished the last of her coffee and stood to leave. Turning to Corey she smiled and added, "You can call me anytime, too."

The door to Corey's bedroom closed. He set down his suitcase and stood motionlessly. He felt lost, homeless, and disconnected. The reality of his situation was again coming back to haunt him. His parents were gone for good. Not out for the evening. Not on some botany field trip. Gone.

Slowly Corey sat down on the bed—another strange bed. How many have there been in the last three months? How long would he be here? How long before he would feel normal again? Corey lay down on the bed and quietly cried.

3
The First Supper

Ellen gave Corey a quick tour of the house. The other bedroom on the second floor was empty, used only for visitors. A bathroom and a linen closet took up the rest of the upstairs.

The living room had a small color TV with rabbit-ear antennae. With luck, the farmhouse pulled in the major networks, although reception was poor. The VCR next to the TV was disconnected, not used for years. Off the kitchen, a hallway led to a bathroom and a small workroom that held a sewing machine. At the end of the hall was Ellen and Ben's bedroom.

As Corey followed Ellen down the basement stairs he noticed the fieldstone walls and the damp smell. A washer, dryer, water heater, and furnace filled almost a third of the clean, single room. Bare light bulbs hung from the ceiling, except for a bank of fluorescent shop lights positioned over a model train set, which was partly covered with a white sheet. Corey noticed it, but before he could ask about it Ben was calling from the top of the stairs. "Corey, grab your coat. I'll show you around outside before it gets too dark."

Ben was a large man. At two hundred and fifty pounds and a little over six feet, he could have passed as a football player. Walking from the house to the barn, Ben and Corey were greeted by Ponch, a ten-year-old border collie. Ben pointed out the property boundaries. "That small cornfield is ours. I rent it out to the neighbor. If you follow the fence line over to the woods, that's ours too."

"What about that big field with pipes in it?" Corey asked.

"That's a center-pivot irrigation system. They're popping up all over the county. We used to own that piece of land, but I sold it when I stopped farming."

Corey felt the mood change a little, and he wondered if he had said something wrong.

The barn contained a workshop and a large storage area. Standing in its center was an old Ford 8N "Redbelly" tractor and the skeletal frame of a Volkswagen Beetle. The attached milkhouse was empty.

The yard light came on automatically, triggered by the darkness of the late winter afternoon. As they headed away from the barn, Ben turned to Corey and said quietly, "I know this is going to be an adjustment for you, but we're both glad you're here." Without another word, they walked back to the house.

"Just in time," Ellen proclaimed. "Now both of you get washed up. We're eating in five minutes."

On the small kitchen table, Ellen had set out three mismatched place settings. A platter in the center of the table held a huge pot roast surrounded by carrots, onions, and potatoes. A wooden salad bowl and a white gravy pitcher took up the rest of the space. "I hope you're hungry," Ellen said.

Corey glanced at the counter and saw a large chocolate cake. Clearly Ellen had worked hard to make this first supper special. But he had not had an appetite in months and still didn't.

"I don't know what your religion is," Ben said, "or even if you have one, but in our home we pray before meals."

Ellen quickly added, "You can just sit quietly if you would like."

Corey nodded.

"Dear Lord, thank you for this meal," Ben said with his eyes closed and his hands folded, "and thank you for bringing Corey to our home so that, with your help, three lives can be made whole again."

"Again?" Corey thought. Logic briefly surfaced and then disappeared.

Ben continued, "Please keep us healthy in mind and body. Amen."

"Amen," Ellen and Corey said in unison.

The meal seemed to go on forever. Corey tried to eat a little of everything but mostly just pushed things around on his plate.

"What do you like to do for fun, Corey?" Ben asked, trying to start a conversation.

Corey was relieved at the question. Finally, someone wasn't prying into his feelings. He hated telling people how he felt. "Not much really. I like to cross country ski in the winter and in the summer I just like to explore. I really like plants…native plants," Corey explained. "I also played a little soccer in the summer when I wasn't on a field trip with one of my dad's botany classes."

"Where did you go on these field trips?" Ellen asked.

"It depended on what ecosystem they wanted to study. I've been to the dunes in Indiana, the backwaters of the Mississippi, and the Boundary Waters of Northern Minnesota. Last summer we went to the Everglades and out to Joshua Tree in California."

"Sounds like you've been everywhere," Ellen said.

"I'd love to get to a rain forest and maybe to Antarctica someday," Corey replied.

The conversation helped move the turmoil in his life to the back of his mind for a few minutes—a welcome break. By the time the chocolate cake was

8

brought to the table, Corey realized that he had eaten a whole meal. The first real meal in months was not enough to make his pants fit better, but it was a start.

Ellen cleared the table and Ben wiped the plastic top with a damp cloth. The dishes were stacked near the sink. "I'll take care of those a little later," Ellen said. "Let's talk a bit." With that, she took a yellow legal pad off the counter. The first page was filled with small, neat, writing. Corey didn't like the looks of this.

"We want you to feel at home with us," Ellen said. "Every home has to have some rules in order for things to run smoothly, and this may seem a little overwhelming, but I don't know of any other way to do it. Feel free ask questions anytime."

"Um-m," Corey murmured.

"Let's start with your room," Ellen continued. "It will be up to you to keep your room clean. You'll make your bed each morning and throw your dirty clothes down the clothes chute outside your room. I will wash and fold your clothes, but it will be up to you to put them away.

"You can use the bathroom upstairs and throw your towels down the chute also. We'll expect you to take a shower or a bath daily and keep your hair neat. The water heater is small, so showers will need to be short." Ellen spoke gently, but firmly.

"We eat our meals together. Supper is at six. On special occasions, there will be snacks around; other than that, there will be no eating between meals.

"You can watch TV as soon as your homework is done and checked. Your bedtime on school nights will be ten o'clock, weekends eleven."

The mention of school sent a wave of fear through Corey. He had forgotten that he would have to deal, once again, with being "the new kid."

Ellen continued. "You will be expected to help with the chores and dishes."

"Do you know much about working with cars?" Ben asked.

"No, but I could learn."

"One thing we insist on is complete honesty," Ellen said in a serious voice. "We need to know that everything you tell us is the truth. If you feel uncomfortable telling us something, you can say 'I'd rather not talk about that' or something along those lines. Does that make sense?"

Corey nodded. He somehow found this arrangement comforting. He could honestly say that he didn't want talk about something.

"You don't have to tell us everything, but we need to know that what you tell us is the truth." Ellen turned a page on the yellow pad. "Let's talk a little about privacy. We use a 'closed door' rule. Simply put, if a door is closed, you knock and wait for permission to enter. If you want privacy in your bedroom or the bathroom, close the door. No one will enter without your permission. Likewise, if our door is closed, you will knock and wait for permission to enter.

Does that sound reasonable?"

Corey thought back to his brief stay with his grandma in January. She still thought of him as a little kid and had a habit of walking in on him when he was in the shower. This "closed door" rule could work out just fine. "Yes, that sounds okay," he answered.

"If you feel better about it, there are locks on both your bedroom and bathroom doors," Ben said.

Ellen quickly added, "Please understand that if I thought for a minute you were in trouble, I'd come through that door, lock or no lock."

Corey looked at this small woman. She couldn't have been much more than five feet tall, but Corey understood that there wasn't a lock in the house that could stop her. He had this vision of her standing in the doorway with the door busted off the hinges. Corey almost grinned.

"The last thing you need to know is that you can talk to us about anything," Ben said. "There has been so much that has changed in your life lately, we just want you to know we're here if you need us."

"You're a growing boy. If you have questions…you know…guy stuff, talk to Ben," Ellen added.

Corey blushed and said, "We had health class in the fifth grade. We learned all about that stuff."

"Great," said Ben, "because I've got a few questions!" They all laughed, which helped to dispel some of the tension in the air.

With the rule-setting session over, Corey went upstairs. He finished unpacking the few personal items that he'd been allowed to bring: a photo of himself with his parents taken last year in the Konza Prairie, a cassette tape that his father recorded for him, and a copy of *A Sand County Almanac*, his mother's favorite book. Most of his possessions were in a storage locker in Madison, along with the entire contents of his family's drafty apartment.

An all-too-familiar uneasy feeling returned. It was a kind of darkness that seemed to overwhelm Corey anytime he was alone. He stood motionlessly in his room. Fighting back tears, he took a deep breath and walked downstairs.

Ellen was sitting on the sofa reading a magazine. Ben was watching TV from the recliner. Corey sat down on the sofa and hoped the evening would pass quickly. After two hours of TV, it was time for bed.

"Tomorrow I'll take you to town and get you registered for school," Ellen said.

The words made a sound like breaking glass inside the boy's head. On top of everything else, he had to deal with another new school. He was sure at some point he would explode. So many things had changed for him and no one understood what he was going through. A little shaken, Corey said good night and went up to his bedroom.

A half-hour later there was a knock on his bedroom door. "Corey, are you still up?"

"Sure, Ellen, come on in."

Ellen walked in without turning on the light. The dim glow from the hall-way left the room bright enough to see, yet dark enough to talk. She sat down on the edge of the bed, pulling the blankets up to the young boy's neck. "They say it's supposed to get cold tonight and I remember that the upstairs sometimes gets chilly."

"I'll be all right."

"If you get cold, there are more blankets in the closet." Ellen started to get up, but paused. She turned to Corey and said, "I just want to tell you that I understand what you're going through."

Having kept it bottled up for months, Corey's stress finally surfaced. "No you don't—you can't! Nobody could understand." Tears began to roll down his face. "I don't want to sound ungrateful, but you don't know what it's like."

Ellen brushed the hair from his eyes. In the darkness of the bedroom, Corey could see that she was also crying. "Why don't you try to get some sleep," Ellen said.

4
Registration Day

Corey was awake by four o'clock. Sorting through the last twenty-four hours had kept him awake until midnight, and now his mind was back at it in the early morning hours. The only good thing that could be said was that this sorting, this urgency to have things make sense, kept him from his emotions. Corey liked logic. He hated emotions. He could control logic; he was controlled by emotions.

What did he know? Ben and Ellen seemed like nice people, but something was puzzling him. He wasn't sure what. He wondered what Ben had meant when he'd said "again."

The sound of a radio told Corey that someone was awake downstairs. Figuring it was no use putting off the inevitable, he sat up in bed and immediately noticed a problem. The bathroom was down the hall from his bedroom and he didn't have a bathrobe. He had never owned a bathrobe, and until now had never given it any thought. At home, he could walk to and from the bathroom in his briefs or a towel. It was no big deal. The only ones who would see him were his parents, but Ben and Ellen weren't his parents, and he wanted a robe. For today, he would risk it. He glanced out the bedroom door and made a quick dash to the end of the hall in his underwear.

The hot shower woke him up. Corey loved long showers. It was something that drove his mother crazy because she said it wasted energy. She could be in and out of the shower in five minutes, but Corey would stay in the shower for a half-hour. That wouldn't be possible here. After about eight minutes, the water was already getting cooler. He stepped out of the shower and looked with disappointment at his image in the mirror. "I'll bet I'm the only thirteen-year-old who still looks like he's ten." Corey thought to himself.

Wrapping a towel tightly around his waist, he ran a hand through his wet hair to brush it from his eyes. Then it hit him; his comb and toothbrush were back in his bedroom. Another peek out the door and another dash down the hall retrieved the needed items. Clean, dry, and filled with a little more confidence, he picked up his things and walked out of the bathroom wearing only a towel.

"Good morning Corey. I was just checking to see if you needed anything," Ellen said, standing on the top step of the stairway.

"Uh, Good morning," Corey said, turning beet red.

Noticing how uncomfortable he was, Ellen said, "I'll talk with you when you come downstairs."

Corey set his things down in the bedroom and thought for a minute. On a note pad that he'd packed, he quickly wrote a note. "GET A BATHROBE." He quickly dressed, made his bed, and threw his dirty clothes down the clothes chute. He had never seen a clothes chute before. "Pretty cool," he thought.

Walking into the kitchen, he could smell bacon frying.

"Do you like scrambled eggs?" asked Ellen with her back to him.

"That would be great," Corey replied. "Ellen…"

"Yes?" She turned to face him, sensing that he was on edge.

"I just wanted to say that I'm sorry…for what I said last night."

"Corey, it's okay. You're under a great deal of stress—and in a way you're right, I can't know how you feel and I should respect that. No one can really understand someone else's pain, but it's also important to know that everyone has pain in their life at some time or another. I wish I could tell you that it will go away soon, but…well, life's not always fair."

Corey didn't know what to make of Ellen's words. He'd sort it out later. He sat down to breakfast. Ellen sat across the table with a cup of coffee. "Aren't you eating?" he asked.

"I ate with Ben before he left."

"Why did he leave so early?"

"He had a short run to Black River Falls. He'll be back by two. He said he wanted to show you around the Barrens before it got dark."

"That sounds great." Corey wasn't completely honest. He wasn't quite sure how to read Ben.

"We have an appointment with the guidance counselors at nine," Ellen said. "They'll get you registered for classes and show you where your locker is."

"I won't have to walk into any classrooms, will I?" Corey said, with a hint of fear.

"No. It's Friday and I told them you wouldn't be starting until Monday."

"Couldn't you tell them that it's already March, so I wouldn't be starting until September?"

"Nice try kid." Ellen took notice of his joke.

"Is there any chance we could pick up a bathrobe while we're in town?"

Ellen shook her head and chuckled. "No problem. While we're at it we can pick up some pajamas for you, too."

"No, that's okay." Corey added with a sheepish grin, "Just a robe would be fine." He thought for a minute about Ellen's offer. Either he'd just admitted to someone he barely knew that he sleeps in his underwear, or she'd witnessed the first of his sprints to the bathroom—or both.

A light snow was falling from the overcast skies as Ellen pulled the Galaxy 500 out of the garage. Corey got in and snapped the seat belt across his lap. The Ford was too old to have a shoulder strap. The car was cold and the heater blew icy air at the windshield as they started the sixteen-mile trip to Richmond. With his head resting on the frigid side window, he watched in silence as the view alternated between snow-covered potato fields and jack pine stands. "How much longer before the snow is gone?" Corey wondered to himself. Madison was only an hour and a half south, but he was sure the snow was usually gone by mid-March.

Ellen turned on the A.M. radio. Corey recognized the voice of the public radio host. He thought his parents were the only people on earth who could listen to that boring stuff. He had a theory: they hired someone to take a survey to find out what people care the least about and then they find a guest who can talk for hours on the subject. Then the six people who know the station exists take turns calling in to talk to the guest. Just for fun, the host cuts off a caller or two.

"Remind me to ask what time the school bus comes past the house," Ellen said absently.

Corey went numb. He'd never figured he'd have to ride a school bus. Having to walk into all of those new classrooms was going to be bad enough— but a school bus! What if there was no place to sit? What if he sat in a seat that belonged to some high school kid with a bad attitude? He took a deep breath. "Relax," he told himself. "You can deal with it on Monday. Just sit near the bus driver until you get a feel for who sits where." Corey sat back in his seat. He really wanted to be somewhere else right now—anywhere else.

Located on the outskirts of town, John F. Kennedy Junior High School looked like any other school built in the early seventies. A single story, it was composed of red brick and few windows. Corey took a deep breath as Ellen parked the car in the visitor's lot. "It will be just fine," Ellen said. They got out and walked in the front door. Turning left, they quickly made their way to the office. Corey felt nervous and thought it was a good thing that Ellen knew her way around.

15

"May I help you?" asked a pleasant woman behind the counter.

"I'm Ellen Raine and we have a nine o'clock appointment with Mrs. Conley."

"I'll let her know you're here."

Corey looked around. It looked like, well—a junior high school office. This would be his fourth school in as many months. His grandma had transferred him to a school near her house in Madison shortly after the accident. Two months later, she decided she was too old to take care of a thirteen-year-old. Dropping in on his Uncle Jeff in Dodgeville lasted only long enough for him to learn his locker combination. After Jeff lost his job, it was only a few weeks before Corey was out the door. Now he was here in Richmond. He wondered if he would be around long enough to even find his locker.

"Ellen! Great to see you again. How are you doing?" Karen Conley, the guidance counselor, was in her mid-forties and the only adult in the building more active than the kids.

Ellen introduced Corey and he stepped forward to shake the woman's hand. He didn't say anything; he just nodded.

"Well, Corey, it's great to meet you," Karen said. "I was just looking over your records. You seem to be quite the student. Let's go down to my office and get you set up with some classes." Ellen looked reassuringly at Corey and gently put her hand on his back, encouraging him to follow the counselor. Ellen followed closely behind.

Karen Conley's office contained a large collection of neat stacks of papers. Piles covered every horizontal surface—the desk, the windowsill, the floor. She removed books from the two extra chairs for her visitors. The walls were covered with photos of students. A small marker board had a note written in large green letters. It said, "Thanks Mrs. C, Mom and I are working things out." The note was signed "K. P." Other notes, cards, and artwork, hinted at the strong bond she had with her students. It was clear by looking around the room that Karen Conley loved her job.

A photo on the desk caught Corey's eye. It was a picture of Mrs. Conley and a man whom, Corey assumed, was her husband. It was the background that he recognized. "That's Parfrey's Glen, isn't it?" Corey asked, pointing to the photo.

"Yes it is," said the surprised counselor. "That's my husband and me. How did you know where the picture was taken?"

"I recognized the cobbles in the canyon wall. My father did some work there for the state two years ago."

Karen was impressed. She turned to Ellen and said, "I'm sure you know that we've already started fourth quarter. We can get Corey into all of the year-long courses, but it would be hard to fit him into many of the nine-week exploratory classes."

Ellen nodded. Corey sat in silence, looking like a deer frozen in the head-lights of an oncoming truck.

Mrs. Conley continued. "You'll have pre-algebra, biology, and then a study hall in the morning. In the afternoon we have you in art, world cultures, English, and PE. Homeroom is at the end of the day. Your homeroom teacher is Mr. Culex. He's also your biology teacher. That means you have one less teacher to remember."

There was a knock on the door. Megan Kilman, a ninth grader and the president of the student council, stepped in. "Sorry I'm late, Mrs. C. I'd explain why, but you'd just get mad," she said through her wad of blue chew-ing gum.

"Not a problem. I'd like you to meet Corey. He'll be starting here Monday."

Corey's eyes opened wide for the first time all day as he saw the attractive fifteen-year-old. Ellen recognized that look and tried not to think about what she might have to deal with. "I'd like you to give Corey the grand tour and then help him find his locker," Mrs. Conley said.

"Cool," was her reply.

As Corey walked out of the office with Megan, his hormones were keeping his logic locked up in the basement.

"So, you're in the seventh grade?" Megan asked, while chomping on her gum.

"Yeah."

"You'll like it here. It's a small school, but we have a good time."

Corey didn't respond. Even walking with this cute girl wasn't enough to keep him from looking at the hundreds of new faces sitting in the classrooms. Most of them stared back at him.

Back in the guidance office, Ellen and Karen got caught up on old times. "How are things working out so far?" Karen asked.

"He's only been with us for a day, but so far so good," Ellen replied. "I'd forgotten all about this adolescent hormone thing, though."

"Relax, I'll keep an eye on him for you. He's had some pretty rough breaks lately, but I think he'll do just fine."

"Thanks, we'll take all the help we can get."

Corey and Megan returned. The tour seemed to have eased some of Corey's apprehension. "Thanks for showing me where my classes are, Megan."

"No problem. See ya around."

"Cool."

Ellen stood to leave.

"It was nice to meet you, Corey," Karen said. "On Monday, I'd like you to come straight here. I'll get you to your first class. Now, go home and relax."

Those were two words Corey didn't use much any more: "relax" and "home." The first was too hard to do and the second was gone for good.

As promised, Ellen and Corey stopped at Shop Rite, the local department store, to buy a bathrobe. Ellen held up a pair of flannel pajamas and said with smirk, "Are you sure you don't want...?"

Corey's expression turned from a grimace to a grin. Shaking his head he answered, "No."

The ride home was quiet; Corey was deep in thought. There was so much he wasn't sure of, but he was beginning to think that Ellen and Ben were all right. Within the first twenty-four hours at both his grandmother's house and his uncle's small apartment, he knew he was a burden—in fact, he was told that he was. Ben and Ellen were different. They had been going out of their way to show him that he was welcome. How long that would last was still an unknown.

5
Teachers Lounge

Ed Culex was eating his lunch when Karen Conley came rushing into the teachers' lounge. "There you are Ed. I've been looking for you!"

"Been here all hour, and if I didn't think the little brats would find me, I'd stay here all day." A large stack of freshly photocopied worksheets sat on the table in front of him. Six videotapes sat just to the left of the pile of copies.

"I see you've got this month's science lessons all set," Karen said, only half kidding.

"Well if you wouldn't load my classes with every loser in the seventh grade, maybe I could do some real science for a change," he snarled.

Karen thought to herself, "I can think of one loser I'd like to see out of your class." It was a view that more than a few others shared. Ed Culex used to be a great teacher, but ten years of teaching junior high had taken its toll. Every year he requested a move to the high school and every year he was denied. He taught the same thing each year in exactly the same way. His 16-millimeter films had been transferred onto videotape, his ditto masters had been photocopied, and his biology texts, copyright 1975, had all had their spines duct taped. Three times he refused new textbooks because "nothing much has changed in biology."

The contrast between him and Viola Williams, the other science teacher, who was also eating lunch, was dramatic. Viola had been teaching science for 23 years and was as energetic today as the day she started. Her students were always doing things—peering into microscopes, using computers, taking canoe trips, playing games and, at times, working from the textbook. Last year she was featured in a national educational magazine for a lesson she'd created that had students working in the community to solve environmental problems.

There was another major difference between Viola and Ed. Viola's students respected her. Ed Culex's students feared him.

"Well, Ed, looks like you have a new student in your second-hour class. His name is Corey Nelson," Karen said.

"Oh, great—new kid, middle of the school year. I'll take a guess it's not a corporate move that brought his wealthy parents to town."

"Nice try, Ed. He's Ellen Raine's new foster kid. I met him this morning. I think you've got a winner here."

"Yeah, right! How many schools has he been in so far this year, three?"

"Actually, this will be his fourth, but if you read his file, you…"

"I've heard enough. This kid is a loser and you know it. He should fit in real well with the rest of my cerebral powerhouses."

"I'm telling you, Ed, if you just read his file…"

"Here's the deal, I'll give him a chance, but if he screws up just once, he's history."

"It's good that you're so open-minded. Read the file!" Karen left the lounge disgusted. If there was any way she could have kept Corey out of Ed's biology class, she would have, but this late in the school year it was a formidable task to arrange a schedule for new students.

6
The Barrens

Ben was home when Ellen and Corey returned from town. "Hey! How did it go?" he asked.

"So far, so good," was Corey's less-than-enthusiastic reply.

"Any trouble getting into classes?" Ben asked.

"Karen had everything set for us," Ellen said, putting the registration papers she had to complete into a brown expandable folder labeled "Corey."

"How's Karen doing? Is her husband still working for the county?"

"She's doing fine," Ellen said. "She says to say 'Hello'. She wants us to get together sometime." This went without comment from Ben, which Corey noticed.

"Are you ready for a quick tour of the Barrens?" Ben asked, turning to Corey.

"Sure."

"Grab your coat and we'll go. It'll be getting dark soon, so we'd better make tracks." Ben reached for his enormous brown canvas coat.

Low clouds hid the sun as they walked to Ben's pickup. They drove south down Pine Road for a mile and a half. A quick left had them heading east on Lapham Avenue. Not more than a half mile later they passed a massive wooden sign that read, Mary G. Lincoln Wildlife Area. Ben slowed the truck down.

"Who was Mary G. Lincoln?" Corey asked.

"She was a biologist; an ornithologist, to be precise. She came here with her husband in the twenties. She spent most of her life here in Central Wisconsin working with grassland birds. When most of the early farms in this area failed, she talked the state into buying the land for wildlife. If it weren't for her, this would all be in center-pivot irrigation right now."

Ben let out the clutch and the truck started to roll forward. Vast open spaces could be seen on both sides of the road. Corey guessed that he could see at least ten miles in all directions. "This is almost like being in North Dakota," Corey observed.

"Don't let the view fool you," Ben said. "Much of what you see off on the horizon is privately owned land. Some is used to grow potatoes, the rest of it is just pasture."

The land seemed to be a mix of grasses and shrubs, with a few small stands of oak. Corey saw movement near a bare spot in the field. "Could you stop for just a second?" he asked, urgently. Ben didn't see a thing, but the boy stared intently out the window.

"What is it?" Ben asked.

"Horned larks!" Corey said, sounding genuinely excited for the first time. "They're the first sign of spring. Most people think of robins as the first birds of spring, but the horned larks are—at least that's what my mom always said."

"Your mom liked birds?" Ben immediately wished he hadn't asked.

"Yeah," Corey said quietly. "She used to tease my dad that plants were too stupid to fly south for the winter."

The next few minutes were uncomfortably quiet. Corey looked out the window, thinking of his mother. Ben looked only at the road. "What's that?" Corey asked, pointing to a large dark shape on the distant horizon.

Ben was relieved by the need to answer. "That's a sandstone outlier," he replied.

"What's an outlier?" Corey asked, equally glad the subject had changed.

"Do you want the short answer or the long answer?"

"I'll take the long answer, if we've got the time."

"Time we're not short on," Ben said. "That hill is made of sandstone that was formed underwater, five hundred million years ago, during the Cambrian period. The very spot we are on was covered by a shallow saltwater ocean. As the earth's crust moved around..."

"Plate tectonics!" Corey announced.

"I'm impressed," Ben said. "I didn't learn about that until I went to college. Anyway, as the crust moved, the ocean retreated. For millions of years this area was dry land because it was being pushed upward. Most of the sandstone eroded. That hill, and a few others like it in the area, are all that's left. They are the outliers."

"Cool. Why didn't the glacier wipe them out?"

"The last glacier didn't quite make it this far. This area is called an outwash plain," Ben explained.

"I've never heard of that."

"The glaciers stopped about ten miles east of here. If we were standing here eleven thousand years ago, we'd be looking at a hill of dirty ice that could be almost a half of a mile thick. As it melted, this whole area turned into a huge lake we now call Lake Wisconsin. That outlier would have been an island in the lake."

"Wow," said Corey. Ben had forgotten how teenagers expressed themselves in single words.

"All the sand in this area was brought in by the melting ice."

"That makes sense—I guess."

The sun was dipping low on the horizon. The trip back was silent, and Corey was again deep in thought. As they pulled into the driveway, Corey said, "Thank you."

"No problem," Ben said, "I thought you might like that place."

Corey quickly said, "No. I mean thank you for...well...just thanks."

Without making eye contact, Ben said, "You're welcome."

7
The Dam

"Ben tells me you're quite the birder," Ellen said, as the three were eating supper.

"Yeah," Corey said, shrugging.

"I was thinking the three of us could go for a ride tomorrow," she suggested. "Maybe we could head over to the river. We used to go there a lot in the spring."

"Could be fun," Ben added. "What do you think Corey?"

"Sounds like a good idea," Corey said, offering nothing more than his usual adolescent word conservation.

Morning came quickly. Corey slept through the night, something he had not done for awhile. The stillness of the morning allowed the darkness to return to his thoughts, but only briefly. He was shaken out of his private gloom by the sound of the radio in the kitchen. "Public radio—again!" he thought to himself.

"Good morning," Corey said to both Ben and Ellen as he walked into the kitchen sporting his new bathrobe.

"Well, good morning Corey," Ellen said. "Nice robe, but I kind of liked the towel."

Ben, caught off guard by the comment, laughed while sipping his coffee. The warm liquid slashed up his nose and over the table. Coughing and still laughing, he said, "Give the kid a break, will ya!" Ellen threw a dish towel at him. He wiped up his mess. Turning to Corey he added, "Didn't know she was so mean, did you?"

"This meanie is packing the picnic lunch for both of you, so you'd better be nice to me," Ellen said.

"How far away is the river?" Corey asked.

"Not far, but we're going to the dam at Bittburg. I think you'll like it there," Ben said. "The weatherman said it could hit 40 degrees today. For March, it's a heat wave!"

"We could climb Roche-a-Cri if we have time. It's a great view from the top," Ellen said.

"Better dress warmly then, because it's going to be cold up there," Ben advised.

The drive west to Bittburg took a little over an hour. Along the way, Corey noticed that the fields seemed to be losing snow to the warm weather. This was a hopeful sign. Another hopeful sign was that the truck radio was not on the public station.

The town of Bittburg contained only a bar, a gas station, and a county park that offered a view of the dam. The public parking lot was filled with cars. That didn't make sense to Corey. Why would there be any cars here, let alone a parking lot full? There was nothing here. Was life in this county so boring that people needed to watch water fall over a dam?

Then Corey saw the eagles, at least twenty of them. It looked as if every tree had one or two perched in its upper branches. Most of the birds had white heads, which told Corey that they were at least five years old. A few were all black. They were the juveniles. His mother had said that if you saw juveniles, the population was in good shape. There was a time when DDT, passed through the food chain, made eggshells too thin and no birds hatched successfully. Seeing juvenile birds was one way to monitor the population. DDT had been banned in the US because of the harm the insecticide had caused to other living things, but it was still used in many parts of the world. However, another threat to wildlife in this country was the loss of habitat which could once again threaten the population.

"You knew they'd be here, didn't you?" Corey asked, looking from Ben to Ellen. The delighted look on his face told both of them that coming here was a good idea.

"We had an idea they'd be here, but you can never know for sure. It's really weather dependent," Ben explained.

"Would you mind if I tried to get closer?" Corey asked.

"People aren't allowed over near the trees," Ellen said. "The town protects the birds like they were a local treasure. In a way, I guess they are. They bring in tourists all spring."

"How about if I cross the bridge and go along the east side of the river? They seem to be flying low over there," Corey asked.

"I'm sure that would be okay with the locals. Be careful near the water," Ellen said.

Corey took off down the path that led to the sidewalk and then to the large rocks along the eastern bank of the river. The sun was still high in the sky and felt warm on his face. He found a dry boulder that seemed purposely carved out as a seat. It had the added advantage of being hidden from view, and as

26

such, out of the wind.

Corey settled in to watch the eagles. Brought together by the food that the open water provided, they formed one of the largest congregations of eagles outside Alaska. They seemed to be taking turns leaving their perches and foraging for food. Corey found their five-and-a-half-foot wingspans breathtaking.

He studied the birds as they floated on the wind. He blocked everything else out of his mind, except the thought that his mother would have loved seeing this. The eagles' effortless flight seemed to be carrying away some of the darkness that had surrounded his soul. Time stood still—or at least went on without him. Corey focused on an adult eagle that was spinning large circles high above the river. This lone bird came closer with each circle it completed. Corey watched with increasing intensity as the eagle continued its descent. He could make out the individual feathers on the enormous wings. On the next pass, he could hear the wind rushing over the flight feathers. The bird made a steep banking turn and reached out with its powerful legs. Corey watched in amazement as the bird landed on a granite boulder five feet above his head. The eagle stared at Corey. Corey stared at the eagle.

"You'll never really be alone, Corey," he heard the eagle say. Corey was overcome by fear. Either he was losing his mind or the eagle had just spoken. Logic kicked in. Eagles do not speak. It was just the sun—that's it, too much sun. The wind picked up and the eagle few away. Instead of returning to the roosting trees, it flew east, away from the river. Corey didn't move until the large bird was only a speck in the sky.

The stunned boy got up and walked back to meet Ellen and Ben. On the way he struggled to make sense of what had just happened. Logic tried to guide him. Maybe he was missing his parents—maybe it was just stress. Logic was falling a little short today. The next best thing was to bury these thoughts so deeply that he would never have to think about them. That burial space was getting crowded lately.

"Hey, You must have gotten an incredible view of that eagle," Ben said.

"Yeah."

Ben couldn't understand the response. He'd just seen Corey have the encounter of a lifetime with a magnificent animal, and all he could say was "Yeah." He had much to learn, or remember, about being around teenagers.

"It was absolutely amazing," Corey added.

Ben felt a little better.

"Look, it's still too early for lunch. How about if we head to Friendship and have our picnic lunch at Roche-a-Cri?" Ellen suggested.

"It's quite a climb to the top, but I'm game. How about you, Corey?" Ben asked.

"You guys sure were right about this spot; I'll trust you on the next one."

The drive to Roche-a-Cri State Park took less than an hour. The sandstone tower seemed to rise out of the earth with no warning. A narrow road twisted around to the backside of the park. Along the way Ben stopped the truck so they could read a sign explaining the origins of the petroglyphs that had been carved in the sandstone by some unknown Indian tribe. But all Corey could see in the rocks were the messages some vandals had carved. He was a little embarrassed to read them with Ben and Ellen around.

A few wooden tables marked the picnic area. Behind the tables lay the first of three hundred and three steps that took visitors to the top of the outlier. Corey strained to see the top from the car window. "That's pretty high," he said.

"I hope you deal with heights better than I do," Ben offered.

"Oh, you big chicken. These new steps are solid as a rock," Ellen taunted.

Ellen and Corey made it to the top first and were standing at the railing of the observation platform when Ben arrived five minutes later, looking a little shaken. Walking cautiously toward the railing, he looked out at the countryside below. His huge hands clung tightly to rail. From this vantage point, the three visitors could see sixty miles in all directions. Individual clouds cast small, dark shadows that seemed to race across the landscape.

"What do you think, Corey?" Ellen asked.

"Cool."

Ben explained, "Just about everything you see from up here was covered by glacial Lake Wisconsin about eleven thousand years ago."

"Does that mean this place was an island in the middle of the lake?" Corey asked.

"Yeah," came Ben's single word reply.

"Let's head down for lunch. I'm starved," Ellen said.

After making their way down the long stairway, sitting to eat lunch seemed like a treat. Corey loved the turkey sandwiches, Ellen thought the coffee was great. As Ben was putting the cooler into the back of the truck, Corey asked, "Can we go back up for a little while?" Ben and Ellen looked at each other.

"Why don't you go and we'll wait here," Ben offered.

"Be back in twenty minutes, okay?" Ellen added.

The thirteen-year-old ran to the stairs while the "forty somethings" sat at the table and felt like "fifty somethings." Neither of them said a word, but they knew what the other was thinking. Corey was the best thing to happen to them in almost eight years.

At the top of the stairs, Corey looked out at the horizon. His fears and darkness were being kept at bay—for now. A steady cold breeze blew against his face. Looking down at the parking lot he could see Ben and Ellen. He liked them. Somehow he had just figured that out. He liked Ben and Ellen, and it didn't feel like he was betraying his parents. The rest of the world was too hostile to think about right now, so he wouldn't.

Looking to the north, Corey could make out the clear silhouette of an American bald eagle. This was just a coincidence. It could not be the same eagle he saw at the dam, and besides, that hadn't really happened. Corey walked back down the three hundred and three steps without giving the eagle another thought.

8
The Bird Feeder

Sunday morning followed another good night of sleep for Corey. No loneliness. No emptiness. No talking birds.

"Ben and I will be heading to church at eight," Ellen said, as he walked into kitchen. "I guess that's something we forgot to talk about. You're welcome to join us, but it's okay if you stay here."

Corey hadn't given it much thought. He had been raised as a Lutheran—more or less. He remembered going to Sunday school when he was younger and sitting in the church pew with his parents. But as he got older they seemed to go to church less and less. There was always something else happening on Sunday. He knew he believed in God, but beyond that he wasn't quite sure. It was like the title of one of his dad's favorite songs, *Still Haven't Found What I'm Looking For*. Corey thought about the time his father got into a heated discussion with two well-dressed people who came to the door of their apartment. They said that his dad would be going to hell because he believed in evolution.

"Sure, I'll go to church with you."

Church service was what Corey had expected. The organ was too loud and the people sang too slowly. On the way out, Reverend Olsen was standing at the door shaking each person's hand. His wind-blown gray hair framed the thickest glasses Corey had ever seen. "Good morning Ben, good morning Ellen," he said. "Who is this fine young man with you this morning?"

"Reverend Olsen," Ben said formally, "I'd like you to meet Corey Nelson. Corey, this is Reverend Olsen."

Corey reached out his hand. Reverend Olsen surprised Corey by giving him a hug instead. Not a quick hug, like when he used to visit his grandma on weekends, but a long hug—long enough to make Corey feel a little self-conscious. "It's good to meet you, Corey. I can't tell you how glad we are to have you here." Turning to Ellen and Ben, Reverend Olsen said, "This was the right time. I'm happy for you."

Corey felt like he had walked into a theater and missed the first half of the movie. There was something he wasn't being told. Before he could figure it out, Ben interrupted his thoughts.

"Hey, let's stop by the bakery on the way home and grab some dough-nuts."

"Works for me!" Corey said.

The drive home seemed to go quickly. The air had a spring-like feel to it as they stepped out of the car. It looked like the warm weather would be hanging around for yet another day.

"As long as it's not bitter cold outside, why don't you help me put up a bird feeder on the clothesline post?" Ben asked.

"Sure, but could we wait until we find out if those doughnuts are any good?" Corey replied.

Ben laughed and they went in the house.

It seemed a little odd to be putting up a feeder so late in the year. Many people stop feeding the birds by April. Corey remembered how his mother would make a point of taking down all the feeders and washing them each spring. She was always concerned that in the warmer weather, diseases could be spread from bird to bird. She would also point out that the birds really don't need the feeders. They would do just fine without them. She had said that the only reason people feed birds is to get a better look at them.

The Raines' feeder was handmade. A wooden platform had an opening to hold an upside down gallon cider jug full of sunflower seeds. A larger platform hung below the mouth of the jug to catch the seeds. Corey liked the simple design of the feeder. He never understood how people could spend money on those plastic feeders made to look like barns. It seemed as if they liked look-ing at the feeder more than looking at the birds. His mother's feeders had been a strange collection of wooden boxes, hanging tubes, and wire cages to hold suet. Two years before, he had helped his father pick out a birthday present for her. It was a microphone connected to a speaker in the house that let the sound of the birds be heard indoors. She loved listening to the birds so much that Corey had to listen to his fathers' albums with headphones on.

Ben stood on a ladder he'd stuck into the crusty snow while Corey held the feeder from underneath. Working on keeping his balance and hitting the nails, Ben struggled to attach the feeder to the top of the wooden post. Corey did his best to steady the ladder with his feet and keep the feeder centered on the post with his hands. He also thought about which way he would dive if the ladder fell. Ben would hit the snow. Corey, on the other hand, would be on the receiving end of a flying hammer.

Ben drove in the last nail as Corey noticed the small writing on the under-side of the feeder. Written in pencil, it said, "B+ Nice work."

9
The New Kid

"Are you sure you don't want me to come in with you?" Ellen sat in the car with Corey outside the school. Kids were coming and going in all directions. A snowball hit the car next to them as three kids piled out.

"No, I'm okay." Corey lied.

"Remember to see Mrs. Conley. She'll get you to your first class."

Corey got out of the car. That dark feeling was coming over him again. He wanted his parents more right now than he had for weeks. Trying not to make eye contact with anyone, Corey entered the school building and walked down the hall to the guidance office.

"I'm Corey Nelson. I need to see Mrs. Conley,"

"She'll be out in just a minute," said the secretary with a smile. "Why don't you have a seat."

Corey sat down. In the chair next to him was a kid with a ring in his nose and the hair shaved from half his head. Corey thought the kid was trying to look tough. He didn't have the heart to tell him that he looked like an honor student compared to the kids Corey had seen every day on State Street, in Madison.

"Hey Corey, come on in," Karen said, poking her head through the waiting room doorway. In her small office with the door closed, she asked, "Okay, honest answer—are you nervous?"

Corey inhaled deeply. "Just a little."

Karen waited.

"Well, maybe more than just a little," he admitted. A bell rang. Corey knew what that meant. He would be walking into his first-hour class after it had started.

Karen and Corey walked down the long hallway to his math class. After being introduced to Mrs. Burns, Corey walked into the room. Every student turned to look at him. He wanted to run, but there was no place to go. "Why don't you have a seat here, Corey," Mrs. Burns said.

Corey sat down at a table with three other students. He didn't say a word.

Mrs. Burns handed him a math textbook and then announced to the class, "It's tough to be the new kid in class. My father was in the military, so I know what it's like. So, Corey, I promise I won't make you stand up in front of class and tell us about yourself." The students laughed and then quickly quieted down.

"Thanks," Corey said quietly. He knew right away that he'd be "safe" in this room.

"Why don't the rest of you get out your projects," Mrs. Burns said as she sat down next to Corey. "Look," she said quietly, "I'm not sure what your math background is so you'll just have to wing it for this week. We have a quiz each Friday. You'll take this Friday's quiz, but I won't grade it." Then she added as she rose, "Unless you do really well on it."

"Sounds fair to me," Corey said.

"Hi. I'm Charlene and this is Holly," said the girl directly across the table from him.

"I'm Don, until now the only guy at this otherwise 'male bashing' table," said the stocky kid sitting next to Corey. "Are you new here?" he added.

"Duh!" Charlene said. "What do you think, pin head! It's March. Have you seen him in school before?"

"I just moved here from Madison," Corey said to Don.

"You'll like this class," Don said. "This is the first time I've ever done well in math."

"This is the first time you could even spell the word 'math,' you Bozo," Holly said.

"See what I have to put up with?" said Don with a stupid grin.

"Okay folks, let's get to work. You can brainwash Corey later," Mrs. Burns said sarcastically.

Corey watched as the group built bridges out of dry spaghetti and glue. It was a math lesson unlike anything he had ever seen before. Each team of students tried to build the strongest bridge using the fewest materials. He helped as much as he could.

The bell rang and Corey walked to his next class. Along the way, nearly every seventh grader he passed stared at him. The ninth graders didn't notice him, except for one. "Hey Corey, how's it going." It was Megan, and from the crowd around her, she was extremely popular.

"It's going," Corey said with a smile.

When he walked into his science classroom, Mr. Culex said mechanically, "You must be Corey Nelson."

"Yes sir."

"Well, just stand here for a minute. I guess I'll have to find you a seat."

Corey stood at the teacher's desk as the other students filed in, staring at the newcomer as if he were some lab animal brought in for dissection. "Hey, you're in this class, too?" It was Don. Corey was glad to know somebody in the room.

"I see you have already met my good friend Don. Somehow I knew you two would find each other," Mr. Culex sneered. The bell rang. "Before we begin class, I'd like to introduce a new student. His name is Corey," Mr. Culex said to the class. "Corey, why don't you tell us all about yourself. I'm sure this class would find that quite interesting."

"Nerd!" someone said loudly. The class started laughing and didn't stop for two minutes.

"Well, I see you've gotten the losers all riled up, thanks a lot! Have a seat next to Don over there," Mr. Culex grumbled. "I suppose I have to find you a textbook too."

Turning to the class, the teacher said, "Remember you have your quiz tomorrow. Now pass in yesterday's worksheet as I hand out today's."

Corey looked at the worksheet. Matching cell parts to cell names. How many times had he been required to do this exact worksheet? Oh well. Mr. Culex walked up to where Corey was seated. "As you know," he began, "we are three weeks into the grading period. If you have any hope at all of passing this class, you've got a great deal of catching up to do."

Corey didn't say a word. He was too scared to think about it right now, but he was sure that he didn't like this man. He didn't know why yet, but he knew that he didn't like him.

The rest of the class period was chaos. As Corey completed the worksheet, most of the other students sat and talked. A textbook, and then a folder, flew across the room. Mr. Culex didn't appear to notice. As the bell rang, he shouted, "Your quiz is tomorrow, not that any of you would care!"

Walking out the door with the crowd, Corey felt something—or someone—tugging on his ankle. Losing his balance, he quickly found himself face down on the hallway floor as crowds of students walked by laughing. Getting up, he noticed Mr. Culex standing in the doorway. He had seen the whole incident and hadn't said a word.

Third hour was a study hall for Corey. With no work to do, he signed up to go to the library, thinking it strange how every study hall in every school worked the same way. He walked into the library along with ten other students and took his turn, signing in on a blue-lined tablet at the desk. Like the others, he instinctively walked to the wall of magazines and grabbed a title that interested him.

Bonnie Asio, the librarian, quickly compared the list of students who signed in, with the faces she knew so well. She stopped when she came to Corey's name. Looking across the room, she saw the young boy reading his magazine. That was the first red flag that went up for her. Most of the students who came to the library did so to get out of sitting in a boring study hall. They would take a magazine out of the rack and pretend to read it, or just look at the pictures. This new kid was actually reading. Maybe he just had no one to talk to and this was his way to get through an awkward situation.

As Ms. Asio approached the boy, she was surprised by the title he'd selected: *Audubon*, not *Car and Driver* and not *Sports Illustrated*. That was the second red flag.

"What are you reading?" she asked as she sat down next to him.

"It's an article about the value of prairies in the United States and how they have become the most endangered ecosystem," Corey replied. He suddenly realized that he'd given an answer that was too detailed. It was like when someone asked, "How are you," when they didn't really want to know.

Ms. Asio was impressed. He actually understood what he was reading! The third red flag.

"Interesting!" she said, introducing herself. "It says here that you are Corey Nelson."

"Yeah. This is my first day here."

"How's it going so far?"

"So far, so good."

"You like prairies?"

"Yeah, I guess." Corey added, "My dad was a botanist."

Something about the way he said "was" made Ms. Asio not ask any more questions about his father. Corey noticed this and was relieved. For some reason, he felt the need to add, "My mother was into birds."

"I'm sure you'll like it here," Ms. Asio said. "Let me know if there is anything I can do to help."

"Thanks," Corey said.

Ms. Asio left Corey sitting at the table and walked straight to the guidance office. "Hey, Karen, are you around?" she shouted, walking past the secretary.

"I'm in here, Bonnie." The voice came from one of the small offices down the hallway.

"How could anyone tell," Bonnie said, looking at the piles of file folders that decorated the room.

"What can I do for you?"

"Got any paperwork on that new kid, Corey Nelson?"

"That's Ellen and Ben's new foster child."

"Oh, I heard they had a foster child now. I'm happy for them. No one deserves a break more than they do."

"From the looks of things, Corey could use a few, too." She handed Bonnie a file folder and said, "You'd better sit down before you start to read it."

The rest of Corey's day went without much trouble. There were a few minor goofs that helped remind him that he was the "new kid." At lunch he didn't have a ticket and had to get one from the office. He got lost on the way to art and came in ten minutes late. Also, while going to world cultures, he walked into the wrong room, a ninth grade English class.

But PE was the worst. He stepped out of the shower room to find that there were no towels. He also quickly realized that he was the only one to take a shower, which earned him strange looks and stupid grins from the other kids. A boy from his art class explained, "Seventh graders don't like to take showers here."

"Don't you start to stink?" Corey asked.

"Well, yeah," replied the other student, as if it were normal to stink.

Mr. Taxidea, the PE teacher threw Corey a towel as the bell rang. "I'll write a pass to get you into homeroom late."

Homeroom lasted fifteen minutes. He wasn't sure what he should be doing there. The other students just sat around with their coats and backpacks. They were talking so loudly that they couldn't hear the announcements coming over the P.A. system.

Mr. Culex didn't say a word. Not to him. Not to anyone. The bell rang and everyone rushed out. Remembering his earlier pratfall, Corey waited to be the last one out the door.

The ride home was the last hurdle of the day. Ellen had driven him to school, but he was taking the bus home. Stepping on the bus, he headed straight for the safety of the seat behind the driver. Before he could sit down he heard, "Hey Corey, sit over here."

He turned to see Don waving his hand. Corey gratefully took the seat next to Don as the bus started to roll. "You ride the same bus as I do. Cool!" Don said. "Where do you live?"

Corey was afraid of this question. "I live on Pine Road, down near the Barrens."

"Wow, you're out in the sticks! Why did your parents move way out there?"

"My parents are dead." Corey said quietly. This was the first time he had actually used those words. "I'm living with foster parents."

"I'm sorry," Don said. "My parents are divorced."

For the rest of the ride, Don filled Corey in on how things worked at J.F.K. After thirty minutes of news about which teachers were jerks and which students were "going out," the bus stopped in front of Don's house. The last fifteen minutes of the bus ride seemed to take forever.

Finally arriving at the Raine farm, Corey got out. Ponch greeted him enthusiastically as he walked to the house. He thought about his situation. He knew he was safe and well taken care of, but he also knew that this wasn't his home. The darkness was returning.

"Hi there. How did it go today?" Ellen asked, as Corey walked into the house.

"I guess it could have been worse."

"Sit down and tell me all about it. Did you get any homework? Did you meet any kids?" Ellen was in rapid-fire mode. "Did you have any trouble with the bus?"

Corey let out a quiet laugh. "Slow down! I'll tell you all about it, but I was thinking about walking down to the Barrens before it got dark."

"You're going to walk to the Barrens? That's almost two miles away. How about if I drive you?"

"Thanks, but I think I want to walk. Would that be okay?" Corey asked.

"Sure. Be back by six," she said, and then added, "Be careful."

The walk to the Barrens gave Corey a chance to clear his head. The sky was still overcast, but the air was warm for March. He wanted to forget everything—the eagle, school, and whatever it was that he wasn't being told by Ben and Ellen.

As soon as he got to the large sign that marked the beginning of the Barrens, Corey left the road. A deer trail headed toward a stand of trees, so he decided to follow it.

Along the way he studied the tracks in the snow. His mom had always liked tracks. She would say that the tracks could tell a story. Mouse tracks that ended with a few drops of blood and the imprints from a pair of wings were higher drama to her than anything that could be found on TV. It hadn't snowed for a week, so the tracks were all old.

When he got to the stand of trees, he sat down on a windfall that was just the right height to serve as a bench. If he were here with his parents, they'd be checking the buds for signs of deer browsing or looking for maple "sapcicles." But his parents weren't here. He was all alone and that was just the way it would have to be from now on. He knew his parents would want him to be strong, but he wasn't strong. He was scared. Logic returned. He would fake it. He'd done it before. He wouldn't let anyone know he was troubled. He'd just keep it to himself. No one would understand anyway. Besides, he wouldn't be here long. He didn't know where he would end up, but he knew this was only temporary.

Corey walked quickly home as the sunset faded to darkness. Supper was exactly at six and he spent most of the meal trying to chew between questions from Ben and Ellen. He was honest. He said he liked most of his teachers, except Mr. Culex. He told them about being late for class, walking into the wrong room, and even being tripped in the hall. He didn't mention PE.

After supper he took out the small amount of homework he had. He put a cover on his math book and wrote a summary of an article for world cultures. As promised, Ellen checked his homework carefully. Spelling was his downfall; five spelling errors in a single-page summary.

After an hour of TV, Corey said good night and went up to his room. This was the toughest time of the day for him. He felt alone, and there was nothing to distract him from thoughts of his parents. He picked up the family picture that had been sitting on his nightstand, looked at it briefly, and turned out the light. The stress of the day gave way to exhaustion and he fell asleep.

The sound of the scream brought Ellen running to Corey's room. Ben followed close behind. By the time she had opened the door, he was sitting up in his bed, crying uncontrollably. Ellen turned on the light and put her arms around the trembling boy. Turning to Ben, she said, "I'll sit with him." Ben nodded and left.

"I'm sorry I woke you," Corey said through his tears. Ellen just held him tighter. Short, deep breaths gradually replaced the tears. "I miss them so much," he admitted.

"Just try to relax," Ellen said. Corey slowly calmed down. Ellen reached up and turned off the light. "Do you want me to stay for a little while?"

"Please..." was the quiet response. "When does it stop hurting?"

"It never really does," she said. Ten minutes later Corey was asleep. Ellen closed the door and went back to her room.

10
Revelations

"How are ya Buddy?" Ben asked, as Corey walked into the kitchen in his bathrobe.

"I'm okay," he said, sitting down at the table.

Ben messed up Corey's hair and then poured a coffee cup. "Rough night," he said, as much a statement as a question.

"That was the worst," Corey said.

Ben thought Corey looked empty, like he was trying to block out everything, the good, and the bad. He knew that look well. He'd seen it on Ellen eight years before, and it had really left only in the last few days. He also knew that Corey felt bad about the scene he'd created last night. Ben had no way to tell the boy that his nightmare had helped Ellen more than he would ever know. Corey hadn't seen her leave his room. He hadn't seen the look on her face. She'd become a mother again.

When Ellen walked into the kitchen, Corey looked up. She was the first person he'd allowed to glimpse the emotions he had locked away. Quietly he said, "Thanks for last night."

She walked over to him, rubbed his back, and said, "Hang in there, kid." Nothing more was said. Corey appreciated that. He headed upstairs to get ready for school.

After a quick breakfast, he was out the door to meet the school bus. The clear night left the morning air surprisingly cold. It was 14 degrees as Corey got on the nearly empty school bus. Fifteen minutes later, Don boarded the bus and sat next to him.

Math class went without incident, but science class started poorly. As he walked in the door, Mr. Culex handed him a stack of fifteen worksheets. "Here, these should get you ready for the quizzes you missed." The stack felt heavy in Corey's hand. He just looked at Mr. Culex and sat down.

"Put your things away, class. It's time for the quiz." Mr. Culex handed out a quiz to each student, including Corey, who wasn't sure what to think. He hadn't been there for any of the material. How could he be expected to take the quiz? He looked at the paper as it sat on the desk in front of him.

Mr. Culex was standing above him, looking down. "What seems to be the problem, young man," he said.

"I wasn't here for any of this. I can't take the quiz."

"You had the book overnight. You knew there would be a quiz. I don't see a problem here. Do you?"

"That's not fair!" Corey said, a little louder than he'd intended.

Mr. Culex exploded. "How dare you say that I'm not fair! You drop in here in the middle of my course, from God only knows where, and you expect to be pampered like some little kid. Well, I'm sorry. If your parents cared about your education, they would have kept you in one school at least until the year ended. So you want to talk about fair, go talk to your folks. Now shut up and take the quiz!"

Corey was in a state of shock. He struggled to listen to logic, but all he heard was, "Get Away!" It may have been the wrong move, but he stood up and walked toward the door without saying a word.

"If you walk out that door, don't even think about coming back."

Corey walked out into the hall. He didn't know where he was going, he just knew he wasn't staying. Before he could get to the corner, he walked into a fast-moving woman carrying a huge stack of papers. It was Mrs. Conley. "Corey! What are you doing out here?" she asked.

Before he could answer, Mr. Culex shouted from his doorway, "I called the office. They're expecting you!"

"I think you had better come with me," Mrs. Conley said.

Sitting in the guidance office, Corey reluctantly told the whole story to Mrs. Conley. He noticed that she didn't seem surprised.

"Look," she said, "You shouldn't have walked out of class. I'll straighten things out with Mr. Culex, but you need to promise me that you're going to stay put from now on."

"But he..."

"No buts! You stay in class. Will you promise?"

"Yeah."

"Why don't you hang out here until the bell rings and then go to your third hour class."

Third hour had him back in the library, and back in his magazine. Ms. Asio smiled as he came in and said, "Hey, there he is. How's it going?"

As if on cue, Mr. Culex walked into the library carrying Corey's books.

Dropping them loudly on the table in front of the boy, he said, "You forgot these. By the way, you flunked your quiz. Now there's a surprise!" Mr. Culex walked out.

Corey looked at Ms. Asio and then at his magazine. He closed the magazine and stared out into space. Darkness was returning.

The rest of the day went better. He had a lunch ticket and made it to all the right rooms at all the right times. In PE towels were set out, though he was still the only one to use them. In homeroom, he felt as if he was invisible. No one said a word to him and Mr. Culex didn't look up from his desk once.

After an uneventful bus ride home, Corey asked Ellen if he could go back to the Barrens. She said yes and he took off down the road as fast as he could walk.

As he entered the vast wildlife area, his spirits seemed to lift slightly. Nothing here reminded him that he was the new kid. He flushed a prairie chicken from a stand of trees. This was enough to shake the gloom from his head. Exploring further, he watched a northern harrier hawk skim the snowy ground for mice. At times he just stopped and listened to the wind. When the sun was getting low he started the walk back home. Before he turned onto Pine Road, an old Chevy Blazer passed him with what looked like a TV antenna sticking out of the roof. He made a point to ask Ben about that.

Arriving home just before supper, he had only enough time to wash up and sit down to eat. Unlike the night before, there was no talk of school. Oddly, there was little conversation at all. After helping to clear the table, Corey began to walk out of the room. Ellen said, "Corey, please sit down. We need to talk." Corey sat. "Mr. Culex called from school tonight. He said he kicked you out of his classroom today."

"He didn't kick me out, I walked out," Corey said anxiously.

"You what? You just got up and walked out?" Ben asked.

Corey looked frightened. "He was saying things about my…"

"I don't care what he was saying," Ellen said. "You can't just decide to leave his classroom. I understand that things are a little rough right now for you…"

Corey stood and said angrily, "You don't understand! You can't understand. You don't know what it's like there. You've never had a kid in junior high." As the words were leaving his lips, logic hit him in the chest so hard that it knocked the breath out of him. He wanted those words back. The immediate look of hurt on Ellen's face confirmed what logic had just revealed to him.

How could he not have seen it? Ben saying "again," the sheet over the train set, the B+ bird feeder. There had been another child who lived here, and he, or she, was gone. Corey now understood the Reverend's warm reaction upon

43

meeting him, Ellen's acquaintance with Karen, and, for that matter, why he was living here, rather than someplace else.

Corey sat down, speechless. A painful silence filled the room. Ellen pulled together her courage and began to speak. "His name was Andy. Leukemia took him from us when he was fourteen. That was eight years ago."

Corey felt the pain he had inflicted with every word Ellen spoke.

Ben sat down next to Ellen, put his arm around her, and said, "It was wrong for us not to tell you sooner, but it's been difficult." Corey could see that the large man was fighting back tears. The boy was not as strong, and tears flowed freely down his young face. He wanted to say he was sorry, but the words couldn't be found. He was afraid to say anything for fear of hurting these people more. He slowly stood and walked to his room.

Corey collapsed on his bed. He usually thought of it as a victory when he unraveled a mystery. Not this time. He wanted to unknow this. He wanted to somehow turn back the clock, but he couldn't.

There was a knock on the door. He knew it was coming. Ellen would say that she was sorry but it just wasn't working out. She would explain how she would call Cindy Dalea in the morning and have her find another place for him, some place where he couldn't hurt anyone. "Let's get this over with quickly," he thought to himself. "Come in," he said.

Ellen came in slowly. "We need to talk." She sat down on the bed. Much to Corey's surprise, she reached out and pulled him close. "Looks like we both had a rough day. I'm sorry I didn't tell you sooner, but I couldn't—it hurt too much to talk about. I think you know what that's all about. Now, if you're having problems with a teacher at school, we'll deal with it." She kissed him on his forehead and said, "better get started on that homework." She stood to leave. Corey looked at her like he wanted to say something, but no words came out.

Night blurred into dawn in a confusing mix of emotions. Guilt, loneliness, and anger took turns keeping Corey from sleep. As the sunrise struggled to light up the room, there was a knock on the door. Corey pulled the blanket up to his neck and said, "Come in."

"Morning," Ellen said with a smile.

"Good morning," Corey answered, sounding confused.

"Look, this is a new day, and you and I are going to start fresh. We need to add one more rule to our list. It's not good enough any more for us to just be honest with each other. I think we need to add some type of 'no secrets' clause."

"I don't get it."

"There were things—important things, that we should have told you. And you should have told us right away that you had trouble in school. No more secrets between us. Do we have a deal?"

"Yeah." Corey said. "Then I guess I need to tell you something," he added in a serious tone. Pulling the blankets down to his waist he said, "I don't sleep in pajamas."

Ellen burst into laughter and shook her head. "I think I already knew that one," she said. "When you get downstairs I've got blueberry pancakes ready to hit the griddle."

"Cool!"

"Oh, and I'm driving you to school today."

"Why?"

"I have a few things to take care of."

11
Full Disclosure

When Ellen dropped Corey off at the front door of J.F. Kennedy Junior High School, he made a quick trip to his locker, and went straight to his math classroom, even though classes wouldn't start for another ten minutes. Corey liked it in the math room because he knew he was safe. It was a sanctuary from the meanness that some kids bring to school. No one would trip him or humiliate him there.

Don came in to drop off his books. "Hey, Corey, come on out to my locker. I have something for you."

Corey followed Don out to the locker. After opening it and digging in his book bag, Don fished out a triangular wedge of paper. "Here," he said, "it's from Kim, that girl who sits behind you in art."

"What is it?"

"Don't be stupid, it's a note. I was going to give it to you on the bus this morning, but you weren't there."

"I'll read it later."

Math class started. The bridge project was almost finished and would be tested the next day. Near the end of the class period, the P.A. came on and all work on the bridge projects stopped.

"Mrs. Burns," said the speaker in the wall.

"Yes," Mrs. Burns said to the wall.

"Do you have Corey Nelson with you?"

"Yes, I do."

"Would you send him to Mrs. Conley's office."

"Sure," the math teacher replied turning to Corey. "You know the way?"

"Yeah."

"Well, it was nice knowing you Corey," Don said with a dopey grin.

"Come on in, Corey," Mrs. Conley said. She looked more serious than he'd ever seen her. Corey sat down and she closed the door. He started to get nervous.

"Your foster mother was just here to talk with me."

Corey shifted in his seat. "Am I being sent away?"

"No, not even close," was the immediate reply. "She just wanted me to fill in some details for you." Corey took a deep breath as the guidance counselor continued. "She told me about last night. I didn't know they hadn't told you about Andy, but I guess I can understand."

Mrs. Conley turned her chair slightly, took off her glasses, then continued. "It was a painful time for all of us. Andy was a great kid. Everybody liked him. He loved sports and model trains. Ben and Ellen were proud of him, and rightfully so. In 1987, when Andy was just fourteen, he was diagnosed with leukemia. He was in the hospital for months and Ellen never left his side. She was away from work for so long, she lost her job."

Corey was listening intently.

"I was lucky enough to be the one to work with Andy to try to keep him from falling too far behind in school. Most of the time, I just sat and listened. That's how your foster mother and I got to be such good friends.

"The medical bills piled up at the same time that the drought hit in 1988. They knew they would have to sell the farm—it was the only way they could get out of debt. Meanwhile, Andy was getting worse and it was just a matter of time. They waited until after his death to sell the farm so Andy wouldn't have to know about it. Some big potato company bought it."

At this point Corey's cheeks were wet with tears.

"The last eight years were tough for them. They pulled out of every organization they belonged to and just shut themselves off from the community. There was a time when they thought about splitting up. Reverend Olsen got them into counseling. I've been after them for years to think about adopting, but they thought it would be too painful. We talked about foster parenting, but they weren't sure about that either—and then you came along. I can't think of a better thing to have happened to them, or to you."

Mrs. Conley handed Corey a tissue. "Look," she said. "I've told you enough. You need to talk to them. Let them know how you feel."

"But I said some awful things. I didn't know…"

"I know Ellen. Not more than thirty minutes ago she was in that very chair telling me how glad they both were that you are part of their lives. Now, if I could only get all three of you fools to talk to each other instead of me, I'd be able to get some work done around here."

Corey smiled slightly. Looking at the clock, he asked, "What period is it?"

"Your science class is almost over, if that's what you're thinking."

Corey nodded and said, "Yeah."

"That brings me to my last question. Do you want me to wave my magic wand and switch you out of Mr. Culex's science class? It would mean messing up the rest of your schedule."

"No," Corey said confidently.

"That's what Ellen said you would say."

"Can I go now?"

"Not quite. Ellen is down the hall in the conference room, meeting with the principal. She would like you to join her there."

"Here? Ellen is still here?"

"No, she's in Zanzibar! Of course she's here. Just down the hallway, on the right."

Corey knocked on the door and walked in. Sitting around a large circular table was Ellen and Mrs. Danaus, the school principal.

"Hi, Corey," Ellen said. "Have you met Mrs. Danaus yet?"

"Hello, Corey," said Mrs. Danaus. "Your foster mother was just telling me all about you." That worried him just a little. "Please sit down?"

As Corey sat down next to Ellen, she caught his eye briefly. That was all it took to tell her that Karen had told him everything.

"Tell me," Mrs. Danaus asked, "how have things been going for you here at J.F.K.?"

Corey spent the next forty-five minutes explaining most of what he had gone through so far. Some things he left out. Mrs. Danaus took notes as he talked and then said, "Thanks, that helps a great deal." Then she added, "Mr. Culex will be down in a minute."

Corey looked alarmed. "What is he coming down here for?"

"We're just going to talk a little—get things back on track," Mrs. Danaus said. When the science teacher walked into the room, he looked at the people sitting around the table and said "Hi" to no one in particular.

As he sat down, Mrs. Danaus said, "Have you met Mrs. Raine? She's Corey Nelson's foster mother."

"It's nice to meet you," Mr. Culex said.

"She is a little concerned about science class. Could you tell us what went on yesterday?"

"Sure, I'd love to," he said. "First, let me say that I commend you on having Corey as a visitor in your house. As I'm sure you have already found out, Corey can be—well, a bit of a hot head."

Corey could feel the table vibrating slightly as Ellen's grip on the edge tightened.

Mr. Culex continued. "As with any troubled child, particularly one as outspoken as Corey, I think strict discipline is our only hope. Don't you agree?"

Ellen's eyes were getting large and she inhaled deeply. Before she could speak, Mrs. Danaus jumped in. "Could you tell us about yesterday?"

"Oh, sure. Corey wasn't ready for a quiz and he stormed out of the room," he said calmly.

Ellen had reached her limit. She raised up out of her chair and leaned as close to Mr. Culex as the table between them would allow. Then she opened fire.

"How can you justify giving anyone a quiz on things you didn't teach!"

Sensing the tone the meeting was taking, he said, "I don't have to listen to this assault," and he stood up to leave.

"Sit down, Mr. Culex," Mrs. Danaus said firmly. He sat.

Ellen glanced at her notes and then continued. "Why did you say 'If your parents cared about your education, they would have kept you in one school,' to a child who lost his parents only a few months ago?" Mr. Culex was stunned and Corey was amazed. How could she have found that out? Those were the exact words Mr. Culex had used.

"Next—What kind of crap do you call this!" She dropped the pile of worksheets onto the table. "If this is what you're passing off as education these days, then maybe it's time you sat on the other side of the desk for a while. Please understand that for these last weeks of school, I will be looking over Corey's schoolwork very carefully. I will expect a weekly note from you and a telephone call anytime you even think about putting a grade less than a 'B' on his work.

"Finally, you need know that Corey is not a visitor in my house, he is a member of my family. I think that at this point you have a pretty good idea of how I feel about my family! Have I made myself clear?"

Mr. Culex didn't say a word; he just stared straight ahead. This was the look Corey had grown to fear.

"Corey, this would be a good time for you to head down to lunch," Mrs. Danaus said. Corey stood up to leave. The smile he got from Ellen carried him through the rest of the day.

Waiting just outside the office door as Corey walked out was Don, who said, "You owe me big-time, Corey."

"Was it you who…?"

"Don't ask!" The two friends walked to the lunchroom.

12
The Aftermath

The rest of the day went smoothly. When classes ended, Corey walked hesitantly into homeroom and sat down. Mr. Culex was sitting at his desk checking papers, as usual, and ignoring everyone as they came into the room, as usual.

Although he had won the first round with Mr. Culex, he knew the fight was not over. He still had to get through six weeks in his class. He still had to take care of the missing work somehow. Corey glanced up from his desk to find that Mr. Culex was looking directly at him. It wasn't the look of hate that he expected, but it wasn't a pleasant look either. With no schoolwork to occupy his time, Corey began looking for something—anything, to serve as a distraction so he wouldn't have to look up and see Mr. Culex.

"The note!" he thought. With all that had happened today, he had forgotten it. He pulled the small triangular wedge of paper from his pocket, unfolded it under the table, and set it on his desk. He began to read...

Hi Corey,

I'm sitting in homeroom with nothing to do so I'm writing you this note. I hope you like it here at J.F.K, I do. Except sometimes it can be so boring! Too bad you got stuck in Mrs. Burns' Math class. She's like the meanest teacher in school. She just throws a hissy if you don't have your textbook covered. Like I have time for that!

If you want, you could meet us at the mall after school. I told my mom that I have to stay late all week to work on a school project. She's so lame! I just have to be back at school by six o'clock so her boyfriend can pick me up. What can I say—I'm good!

Do you have a girlfriend yet? Because if you don't, I think you're kind of cute. It's okay if you do because we can just be friends.

Call me,

Kim

Corey put the note away. He had never had a girlfriend before, but it seemed like just about every guy in the seventh grade at J.F.K. did. He tried to use logic to figure out what to do, but logic was off on a trip somewhere. Far too often lately, logic seemed to be somewhere else. If logic was going to ignore him, he'd talk to Don.

A baseball cap flew out the bus window as it pulled away from the school. "Did you read Kim's note?" Don asked.

"Yeah."

"Well? Are you going to go out with her?"

"I don't know. I'll think about it."

"Think! Why think? If you don't go out with her, Steve will."

"Maybe."

"Don't be stupid! Look, have you ever even kissed a girl?"

Corey looked out the window.

"I thought not," Don said. "Let me tell you how the world works. You go out with Kim, even for a little while, and everyone will think you're cool. After that, you're set for life. If you don't, you might as well plan on eating lunch with the graphing calculator geeks. Even Todd 'the nose-picker' Stipa went out with Kim."

"I'll think about it, okay?"

The two seventh graders said little else for the rest of the trip. Don turned to talk baseball with the kid across the aisle. Corey stared out the window. He had one more thing to get straightened out today. He didn't quite know what to say to Ellen when he got home. More than that, he didn't really know how he fit into the picture back at the house, now that he had a new view of things.

Corey remembered when his father told him about going out to Mount St. Helens shortly after its big eruption. He'd flown to Washington State to study how the ash fall affected plant communities. The biggest problem he'd had was that, overnight, every map of the area became useless. Rivers changed course, roads disappeared, and the top of the mountain had blown all over the state. Instantly the landscape had changed. The world people thought they knew had changed in a matter of minutes. That was how Corey felt right now. Just about the time he had it all figured out, reality erupted and changed everything.

Corey walked into the house as the school bus pulled away. Ellen was paying bills while listening to public radio. "Hi, kid," she said.

"Hi." Corey sat down at the table. "Thanks for coming to school today." He searched for the other words he needed to say, but they couldn't be found.

Ellen just smiled and said, "That's what I'm here for." The look on her face said so much more. It said that she knew what Corey was trying to say and that it was okay. She knew it and Corey knew it. Corey relaxed for the first time all day.

Corey took his now daily trip to the Barrens. The warm weather was slowly turning the snow-covered landscape into a sea of matted dried grass. Only a few spots of snow could still be found. Corey realized that this was only temporary. A six-inch snowfall could come at any time and for a few days again lock the Barrens into a white sleep.

For now, Corey would enjoy the early spring. He noticed the harrier hawks enjoyed it too, because the deer mice that spent the winter safe under the snow were suddenly exposed and unprotected. This was a situation Corey knew well.

As his knowledge of the Barrens increased, Corey seemed to feel more at home there. He began to recognize individual animals. He was sure he was seeing the same deer on each visit as it searched for food in a stand of oak. More than just the animals, it was the place—or maybe the feel of the place—that was becoming a part of him.

His exploration continued for a short while and then he headed home. Along the way he heard, but couldn't see, geese heading north. Spring migrations always made Corey feel good. Soon he would hear sandhill cranes. No other sound had excited his mother like that of sandhills in the spring. Thoughts of spending one cold Saturday morning with his mother each spring on the annual Crane Count filled his head. Normally, thinking of his mother would have made him feel sad, but not this time. Having the cranes back would be like having part of his mother back. Corey stopped several times to listen on the way home. He heard geese, dogs, and a chain saw, but no cranes. He knew it was just a matter of time.

Kim was waiting at Corey's locker when he arrived at school. "Hi Corey," she said through at least four pieces of neon-orange gum.

"Hi." Corey started to work the combination on his locker door.

"Don said you were going to write me a note? Did you?"

"No." He'd have to talk to Don about that one.

"Wanna walk around with me?" Kim said.

"I guess," Corey said. "Where do you want to walk?"

"Just around." With that she took his hand and led him down the hall. Every head turned as they passed. They walked down one hallway and back the other, and then the course was repeated—twice. Kim didn't say a word to Corey during the entire trip. She did, however, make a point to wave or shout to just about everyone else. Corey felt uncomfortable—almost like he was

Kim's new puppy that she was showing off. A warning bell rang that told the students they had one minute to get to class. Corey said "Good bye" and headed to math.

"Corey, you dog you!" Don said as Corey walked into the room. "You had me worried yesterday, but you came through in a pinch."

"We just walked the hall," Corey said in his own defense.

"Face it, you two are going out now and the whole school knows it."

Mrs. Burns switched on the overhead projector to signal the start of class.

Science class consisted of a video that was longer than the class period. It let Mr. Culex start the video and not say a word all period. Third hour in the library was Corey's time to relax. With his nature magazines providing entertainment and Ms. Asio providing protection, this was his sanctuary. His plan was to sit back and read all period—until Mr. Culex walked in and sat down next to him.

"Well, young man," Mr. Culex said quietly, "that's quite a foster mother you've got." Corey was speechless. The man he disliked the most was sitting three feet from him and Ellen was sixteen miles away. The stress in the boy's face brought a feeling of satisfaction to Mr. Culex. It also brought Ms. Asio to the table as quickly as she could cross the room.

"Is this a private party or can anyone join in," she said.

"Mr. Nelson and I were just about to talk about some make-up work," Mr. Culex said, clearly annoyed that Ms. Asio was there.

"Make-up work? Corey, I thought you said you just got here this week."

Before Corey could say a word Mr. Culex jumped in. "We were just trying to figure a way Corey could complete all the work from the start of the quarter. I was thinking maybe a ten-page report on cell division by Friday."

Corey's eyes went wide. Ms. Asio quickly countered, "How about a ten-minute oral report on the subject of his choosing by Monday." Panic was now setting in.

"Sounds good to me," Mr. Culex said and then quickly left the library.

As the reality of what had just happened sunk in, Corey turned to Ms. Asio and said, "Do me a favor—don't do me any more favors!"

"Relax! You can do your work on some ecosystem, maybe prairies or deserts."

"But an oral report?"

"Look, I've seen your spelling scores from your school in Madison. Stick to your strengths."

"I can't do this!"

54

"You can and you will. I'll help; it'll be fun!"

"You have a strange idea of fun. I'll bet you listen to public radio."

Ms. Asio laughed. Minutes later the table was covered with books and magazines. Corey selected prairies and began taking notes. He had to pull this off or else Mr. Culex would win, and Corey would never let that happen.

The teenager walked into the farmhouse with a massive collection of books and magazines. Ben was home early and did a double take when the book bag hit the floor with a thud. "Wow," Ben said. "You were either really bad or really good!"

"I got tricked into doing an oral report on prairies for Monday."

"You actually need books to tell you about prairies? I figured you should be the one writing books on that subject," Ellen said. The telephone rang and Ellen picked it up. "It's for you, Corey."

Confused, Corey took the telephone. He said nothing, but every now and then made a noise that could be mistaken for a word. Ten minutes later he hung up. Ben and Ellen were dying to ask, but didn't. Finally, Corey said, "It was this girl from school, Kim. She says she's going to ride her bike over here on Saturday. If that's not okay I'll tell her not to come over."

"That would be fine," Ben said. "Besides, the weather on Saturday is supposed to be warm, great weather for a date."

"It's not a date! She's just this girl from school."

"My mistake—sorry."

Corey took his books to his room. Ellen looked at Ben and said, "We've been waiting for the right time. I think this is it."

"Yeah, I think you're right."

"You get it out of the barn and I'll get Corey."

"I think it's what Andy would have wanted," Ben said and headed for the barn.

"Hey Corey," Ellen shouted up the stairs. "Come on out to the barn with me. I've got something to show you."

Corey and Ellen arrived at the open barn door as Ben was walking out carrying a used but still shiny bicycle. They didn't need to explain where it had come from—Corey knew in an instant. "We bought it for him when he was your age," Ellen said as she put her arm around Corey. She could feel him beginning to shake. "He used to love to ride it everywhere."

"We think you should have it," Ben said.

"I can't," Corey said, in words that were hard to hear.

"Look," Ellen said, holding the boy tighter, "Andy would have wanted you to have it, and when we see you riding it, it will remind us of some very good times we had with him."

"But…"

"Look, Sunshine, you saw what I did to Mr. Culex. Now if you know what's good for you, you'll get on that bike and ride to the Barrens."

Corey swallowed, said "Thank you," and rode off. His head was spinning with questions as he pedaled down the gravel driveway. How could seeing him on Andy's bike bring back good memories? Wouldn't he just be causing them the same pain he had only yesterday? Wouldn't seeing, or even hearing, the bike make them sad? As he came within sight of the wooden sign that marked the entrance to the Barrens, the unmistakable sound of a sandhill crane off in the distance caused Corey to stop the bike immediately. He now understood.

13
The Date

Corey was working at the kitchen table when Ben came down at 5:30 on Saturday morning to make coffee. "What are you doing up so early?" Ben asked.

"I've got to have this done by Monday."

"It's 5:30 in the morning!"

"I know, but I couldn't sleep."

"Well, how's it going so far?"

"I think I have a rough outline of what I want to say, but I need to be sure I have my facts straight. If I goof up on something, Mr. Culex will jump all over me."

"If you goof up on something," Ben said supportively, "you'll still walk out of the room as Corey Nelson and he'll still have to be Ed Culex. Now, you tell me who comes out ahead."

Corey smiled. "Yes, I know, but I still want to do well."

"Who are you trying to kid? You want to kick butt on this project because Mr. Culex thinks you're going to fall flat on your face."

Another smile. "Well there's that too," Corey said. "My dad had a ton of slides on prairies. Too bad this assignment couldn't wait until next fall. I could get some shots to liven this report up with."

Ellen came down the stairs, confused by the crowd in what was usually an empty kitchen at this time of the morning. "Did I oversleep or are you two just trying to mess with my head?"

"It's that head thing," Corey said with a sarcastic grin. Ellen walked over to him and gave him a hug.

"Good morning, kid. How did you sleep?"

"Okay. I kept having dreams about Asclepias and Monarda."

"Who are they?" Ben asked.

"THEY are prairie plants."

"When I was thirteen I didn't dream of prairie plants!" said Ben, smiling.

"Give me a break," Corey protested. "This is important."

"Sorry Bud, I know it's important to you. Just keep working, I'll leave you alone." Ben turned to Ellen and said, "I've got to make a short run today, but I'll be back by supper."

"You didn't have a run today," Ellen said.

"This one just came up."

Corey worked on his report without getting out of the chair once. Ellen put a plate of pancakes in front of him and he ate it without looking. Scraps of paper littered the floor and books were piled everywhere. Anything that could serve as a bookmark was wedged between the pages to keep some important fact handy. Ellen turned the radio on at seven; it was public radio. "Coming up next," the announcer said, "we'll take a look at the Governor's plans to improve education in Wisconsin."

"Why do you listen to that stuff?" Corey asked.

"Hey! I learn all kinds of new things listening to this stuff," Ellen responded.

"What's the big deal? If you want kids to learn, you drop them off in a prairie and say 'Don't come back until you've learned something.' That's all there is to it."

Ellen laughed. "That was quick. Now can you solve the rest of the world's troubles?"

"Sure, no problem—but can it wait until after I finish this report?"

"How's it coming?"

"Okay I guess."

Corey worked without a break until 10:30. Groaning as he got out of the chair for the first time all morning, he stretched and said, "That's enough for now. The first draft is done!"

"What time is Kim coming over?" Ellen asked. He had forgotten all about Kim and really hoped she would forget all about him.

"She said she would get here around eleven."

"Do you plan on being in your bathrobe when she gets here?" He had been so focused on his report that he had even forgotten to get dressed. He ran upstairs. Ellen heard the shower start as the doorbell rang.

"Hi, I'm Kim. Is Corey here?"

"Come on in, Kim," Ellen said. "Corey will be down in a minute." Kim was dressed in jeans and a sweatshirt, sneakers, and a light jacket. Noticing that Kim's hands were deep red, she said, "You must have had a cold bike ride this morning. How far away do you live?"

"It's about six miles from here. Do you know where the Elmwood subdivision is?"

"Wow, that's quite a ride."

Corey came down the stairs, surprised that Kim was so early. "Hi Kim," he said.

"Hi, Corey. What do you want to do?"

He hadn't given it much thought. The only thought he did give it was to wish it wouldn't happen at all.

"I don't know. We could watch TV or maybe go to the Barrens."

The thought of hanging out with her new boyfriend while an adult was around didn't appeal to Kim. "What's 'the Barrens'?"

"It's this cool place a mile or so from here. There's lots of animals and it's fun to just hang out."

"Sounds like fun." Kim lied. It sounded stupid, but she wanted to be with Corey no matter what it took.

Ellen instructed them to be back for lunch, and they were off. They biked down the road and stopped at the big sign that said Mary G. Lincoln Wildlife Area. "Here we are," Corey said with a hint of pride in his voice.

"There's nothing here," Kim said. "It's just a bunch of dead grass. Where are the animals?"

"You have to sit and wait, but they're around. Sometimes you get surprised by what you see."

"Who was Mary G. Lincoln?" Kim asked.

"She was this really important woman who worked to help wildlife. She spent most of her life in this area studying the birds that need grasslands to survive. She was also real good at getting politicians to see that this place was worth saving."

"Sounds like a strange woman to me. Who would want to spend much time here?" Corey let that comment go without a reply. They set their bikes down near the sign and walked along the deer trail. Kim talked nonstop about school, about who was going out with whom, and about how her mother always yelled at her. Corey tried to listen, but it was difficult. Normally when he was here, no one talked. It's not that it was quiet, there were always sounds, but he didn't have to listen to someone else. He liked the way he could tell what animals were around just by their sounds. Not today. Today he had to listen to Kim.

They kept hiking along the trail until they got to a stand of oak trees. Corey tried to point out birds along the way, but Kim had a difficult time seeing them. A dry windfall made a somewhat comfortable bench. They sat down on the log and looked up at the sky. Kim turned to Corey and asked, "What are you thinking about?"

"Nothing."

"You can't think about nothing. What are you thinking about?"

"I don't know."

"Look, if you're going to be my boyfriend you have to be able to tell me what you're thinking."

Corey wasn't sure he wanted to be Kim's boyfriend, but decided to take her challenge and tell her just what was on his mind. "I was thinking about how people don't know what they've got. People drive by the Barrens every day and have no idea how many different types of plants and animals are here."

Kim was clearly annoyed. She had hoped to hear something more romantic from her boyfriend. "Are you going to kiss me or not?"

"What?"

"Don said that you wanted to kiss me."

Again, he would have to have a talk with Don. "I don't know. I guess." Fear gripped him. What if he did it wrong? On the lips or the cheek? Eyes open or closed? Corey came up with a plan just in time. He would kiss her quickly on the lips and keep his eyes closed. Kim leaned her head closer to him. He had to admit, she was really cute. Maybe this 'girlfriend' thing would work out just fine. He summoned up his courage and leaned forward. Taking aim at Kim's lips, he closed his eyes. The instant before contact, a familiar sound off in the distance caused him to open his eyes. "Cranes!" he shouted. Unfortunately, his kiss inertia couldn't be stopped in time. His loss of concentration landed his lips squarely on the underside of Kim's nose.

"Gross!" Kim said, wiping the saliva from her nose.

Corey didn't hear. He was already down the trail, getting closer to the cranes. Standing four feet tall, the birds alternated between pecking at food in the grass and keeping a watchful eye out for predators.

Corey was filled with a warmth he hadn't felt for a long time. He somehow didn't feel quite so empty. The illogical part of his brain briefly recalled the voice by the dam saying "you'll never really be alone Corey"—an event that he knew didn't really happen. One small part of that event made sense. He understood that he would, in a way, always have his parents with him. They were a part of him—like the Barrens was becoming a part of him.

Kim walked up to Corey ready to yell at him, but something about the way he was watching the cranes caused her to slow down and approach quietly. She sensed a sort of reverence, an almost church-like calm. "What are you looking at?" she said quietly.

"Look over there." Corey pointed to the large brown birds two hundred yards away.

Kim watched the birds and was impressed. Maybe Corey was on to something. Maybe it was okay to have a boyfriend who was a nature freak.

The cranes began spreading their wings and jumping up and down. Their calls were now coming at the same time. Corey knew this as the 'unison' call. One crane picked up grass in its beak and then dropped it. "What are they doing?" Kim asked.

"It's the dance!" Corey whispered. He was thrilled that his girlfriend seemed interested in birds. "They are a couple and they are doing a courtship dance. If they didn't dance, the female wouldn't ovulate and they wouldn't be able to mate." The sound of Kim's hand slapping Corey face was loud enough to get the cranes' attention.

"Corey Nelson, you are disgusting!" Kim said as she stormed away.

"What did I say?" he shouted.

"You're sick and I never want to talk to you again." Seconds later Kim was too far away to respond.

Although startled, the cranes didn't fly away. Corey was confused. The sound of the cranes quickly brought his attention back to the field. He watched for nearly an hour before the cranes wandered off behind some brush.

Hunger and his report on prairies forced him to head home. He walked down the deer trail toward the sign and his bike. He could make out a truck or a car parked next to the sign. It was too far away to see clearly. Corey immediately thought of the unlocked bike. If it got stolen, he wouldn't know what to do. He began to a run until he was close enough to make out the vehicle. It was the Blazer with the antenna sticking out of the roof.

A woman sat behind the wheel as a man was digging around in the back of the car, as if looking for something.

"Hey, cool car," Corey said as he got close.

The man digging in the back of the car looked up. "Hey, is that your bike?" He sounded unfriendly.

"Yeah."

"This isn't a playground for you kids to trash," he said angrily.

"I wasn't trashing a thing," Corey said, defensively. "I was just walking around."

The woman from the driver's seat got out and walked to the back of the car. Ignoring Corey as if he was an unfortunate interruption, she said, "Hey, Steve, did you hear those cranes calling?"

"That was a unison call and they're just on the other side of that stand of white oak," Corey said.

The two visitors were surprised by Corey's knowledge of cranes. "How do you know about cranes?" the woman asked.

"I've been watching cranes as long as I can remember. It gives me something to do when I get tired of 'trashing' the place," Corey added sarcastically.

"Okay, maybe I was wrong," the man said. "How about we start over. I'm Steve and this is Wendy."

"I'm Corey Nelson and I live just down the road. What's with the antenna?"

"It's nice to meet you, Corey," Wendy said. "We're tracking some birds with radio telemetry, so we need to use the dorky-looking antenna to find them."

Corey couldn't help noticing that she was into birds as well as good looking. Maybe she should talk to Kim. "Cool. Are you grad students?"

"Yes we are. We're both in the wildlife program at Stevens Point. How did you know?"

"My dad used to have graduate students working for him back in Madison."

"Your father is a professor?" Steve asked.

"He was an assistant professor. He's dead now. He and my mom were killed in a car accident." Wanting to change the subject quickly he asked, "Are you tracking cranes?"

"No," Wendy said, "prairie chickens. We have three birds fitted with radios and we spend all day keeping track of where they are."

"Cool. Are you going to go find one now?"

"We don't need to. We use triangulation to pinpoint where they are," she said.

"What's that?"

"It's easy, really. The radio can't tell us exactly where a bird is, it can only tell us which direction it's in. So we get a bearing on it from three different points and then draw lines on a map. Where the lines intersect, bingo! We can learn about what type of habitat the birds need at different times of the year without having to trap them. That way the wildlife managers can know how to help the birds survive."

"Cool. But how do you know which bird you're hearing?"

"Here's the tricky part." Steve took over the explanation. "Each transmitter is tuned to a different frequency. We have three birds tagged right now, but we should have four. One of our transmitters is a piece of junk. We can pick a frequency on the receiver if we want to find a specific bird, or we can let the receiver scan all the frequencies if we're just looking around."

"Here," Wendy said as she tossed Corey a walnut-sized object. "Take a look at 'Number Four.' It doesn't work, but it will give you an idea of what they're like." The transmitter was smaller than Corey had expected. "Our supplier is sending us a replacement for that one. We've already told them we got rid of it. Why don't you take it to school and show your teachers?"

"Way cool. Thanks a lot! I'm late for lunch so I've got to get going. Will you be around here again sometime?"

"We're here all spring, and off and on over the summer," Steve said.

"Cool. See ya later."

"Take care, kid."

Corey headed home having lost one girlfriend who didn't care about birds and gained two new friends who planned to make birds their career. He thought about the broken transmitter in his pocket. Maybe he could use it as a prop for his talk to make up for not having slides. Corey heard the cranes once more before pulling into the driveway. Each time he heard them, he knew he wasn't really alone.

"Where's Kim?" Ellen asked as he walked in the door.

"She decided to go home early."

"Is everything all right?"

"Yeah…I guess," Corey said. "Is Ben back yet?"

"He should be back soon. You two are going to have to fend for yourselves tonight. I'm going out."

"Okay," Corey said as he pulled out his books.

"Leave that until later. You need to eat something or you'll starve to death. God only knows what Ben will be feeding you tonight."

"Pizza!"

"I'll leave that up to you two." Corey ate a sandwich and gulped down a bowl of soup. He told Ellen all about Wendy and Steve, and showed her the broken transmitter. Then it was back to the books. Corey was still working at 2:00 when Ben walked in the door carrying a paper bag.

"Hey Bud, how did the date go?"

"It wasn't a date—and not real well." That was all he said about Kim, but he filled Ben in on Steve and Wendy. Ben seemed much more impressed with the broken transmitter than Ellen.

"Must be a guy thing," Ellen said.

"How's the report coming?" Ben asked.

"Okay. I've gotten the first draft done; I'm just working on adding the details. I'm thinking of working the transmitter into the report so I can use it as a prop. I've got to do something to make up for not having any prairie slides."

Ben pulled a package the size of a cereal box out of the bag he was carrying and set it on the table. Corey recognized the handwriting on the slide tray box immediately. "These are my father's slides. How did you…? You drove to Madison to get slides for my report?"

"I called your grandma. She had a key to the storage locker. Can you use them?"

Corey was speechless. Why on earth would Ben have given up one of his few days off to get these slides?

"Thank you. You just saved me a ton of work."

"Does that mean I can pull you away from this report tonight?"

"What did you have in mind?"

"I don't know. Ellen is going out with Karen for some type of 'girls night out,' so I thought we could have a 'guys night' too. I was thinking of heading down to the YMCA. We could shoot some hoops, maybe swim, then grab a video and a pizza and head home."

"Sounds good to me!"

Ellen left at five and the guys headed to the YMCA shortly after. Basketball lasted only long enough to find out that Corey couldn't dribble to save his life. Swimming was a different story. The kid was a fish. Ben could swim well enough to be safe in the water, but he was not going to set any records. Most of their time was spent horsing around in the pool, and twice Ben got "talked to" by the pimply-faced seventeen-year-old lifeguard.

Back in the locker room, Ben said, "We have a great swim team in town. You should think about joining when you get into high school."

"I'd like to, but who knows what town I'll be in when I'm in high school." Corey finished getting dressed, unaware of what he had just said. A wave of panic flashed through Ben. He felt as if he had walked over a frozen pond and heard the ice crack. Ben and Ellen had come to think of Corey as a permanent part of their lives. Corey knew only what he was told by social services—any placement was temporary. Ben shook off his fear as the two of them left the locker room.

The pizza selection was easy, extra cheese, no mushrooms, and no olives. They agreed on that in a minute. The video was much harder to pick. Ben liked westerns; Corey wanted a nature documentary. They settled on some "knights of the round table" video and then an action film about a submarine.

Before the first movie was half over, the pizza was gone, proving much better than the film. "So do I ever get to hear about you and Kim?" Ben asked.

"Not much to tell. She thought we were going out, I didn't. Now I think we both agree we aren't."

"You know that if you ever need to talk about that stuff…you know…"

"I told you, we had that in fifth grade."

"Yeah, and I also know what it was like to be thirteen. Answers you got when you were ten aren't always good enough. Just know that there isn't anything you and I can't talk about."

"Anything?"

"Anything."

"And you won't tell anyone or get mad?"

"I didn't say that. You'll just have to trust me. If you tell me that you're thinking about hurting yourself, I'm not going to sit back and keep my mouth shut. It all comes down to trust. You're free to talk about anything you want. You're also free not to. Deal?"

With that, the floodgates opened. Corey asked questions that were so blunt and honest they took Ben by surprise. Although he'd had the same questions when he was Corey's age, he wouldn't have thought of asking anyone about them. Ben's answers were complete and to the point, leaving no room for mis-understandings. Ben figured that this was no time to be subtle. Each answer sparked new questions. By the time they were done, just about every adoles-cent anxiety and parental fear was addressed. The two had determined where their limits of trust were, and clearly, there were no limits.

By the time the credits from the second video rolled across the screen, Corey was asleep on the floor. Ben woke him up enough to get him up the stairs. He was heading back down to turn the TV off when Ellen came home. "How was your girls' night out?" he asked.

"We had fun. How about you guys?"

"It was a good time. Once you get that kid talking, you can't shut him up."

"Oh, what did you talk about?"

"Just guy stuff."

"Like what?"

"Let's just say that you're living with a very normal teenager."

"Heaven help us!"

14
The Report

Corey spent most of Sunday fine-tuning his report on prairies. He added notes in the margin that told him which slides to show and when. When he was sure he had it down, he presented a dress rehearsal to Ben and Ellen in the living room. With no projector available, they were forced to hold the slides up to the light from the window and view the small images.

Ben and Ellen were impressed. The presentation was articulate, detailed, and interesting. "I'd say you nailed it!" Ben said.

"You're going to do just fine," Ellen offered.

"I think I'm set—just a little nervous. Is it all right if I head down to the Barrens for a while?"

"Sure," Ellen said. "Just be home by six o'clock." With that, Corey was out the door.

Ben picked up the slide tray and started looking at the slides Corey hadn't selected. The tiny images of an active young boy filled most of them; hiding in the tall grasses, standing with outstretched arms on a windy prairie hillside, or asleep under a bur oak. It became clear that this was more than just a collection of prairie slides, it was also a shrine to a child who's father loved him dearly.

Ben showed the slides to Ellen. Seeing Corey as a young child helped them fill in some of the years they had not shared with him. In reality, Corey had been with the Raines for only a short while. As much as Ben hated to admit it, Corey was right—any placement in foster care was temporary. Ben was afraid of how close Corey had become to them. He wondered if it was fair of them to use Corey to fill a painful void in their own lives. Could Ellen deal with Corey's leaving? He knew the answer to the last question and tried desperately to put it out of his mind.

Corey spent the rest of the afternoon in the Barrens, filled with the confidence that his report was done well. The warm weather looked like it was here to stay. Harrier hawks were working the fields and the buds on the shrubs were getting fat.

Off in the distance he could make out the shape of a Chevy Blazer with an antenna sticking out of its roof. He reached into his pocket and took out the broken transmitter Number Four. Looking at the resin-covered electronics, he wondered if the problem was just a loose wire. He squeezed the transmitter tightly and immediately heard the sound of brakes locking up on gravel.

"Cool!" he said out loud, as a cloud of dust lifted from the road in the breeze. The car backed up and Corey started running down the trail.

"Hey, I got it to work!" he shouted as he met the two graduate students at their car. "I just squeezed it real hard and now it works."

"Hey Corey," Wendy said. "Are you an electronics whiz too?"

"I don't know the first thing about electronics. I just squeezed it and I guess now it's fixed."

"Not quite," Steve said. "Let me see that piece of junk." Corey handed him the transmitter. Only then did it sink in that he would have to give it back now that it was working. "Listen to this," Steve said, nodding with his head to the receiver in the car. He squeezed the transmitter and the receiver started to click loudly. When he let his grip relax, the clicking stopped. "Just as I thought, it's got a short circuit." He tossed the transmitter back to Corey.

"Don't you need this?"

"Nope, the replacement is on the way and it would take too long to teach the prairie chickens to squeeze it just right." Corey laughed.

"Hey, Corey, Steve and I were thinking—have you ever been to a booming grounds?"

"What's that?"

"It's where prairie chickens do their courtship display. You'd love it. We sit in a canvas blind while the male prairie chickens put on this awesome show. When a female comes into the area, the place just goes nuts!"

"Sounds like fun!"

"We signed up for a blind for next Saturday. There's room for three, if you're interested."

"Interested? I'd love to go. What time?"

"We need to be in the blind at four-thirty A.M. That way the birds don't freak out when they see us."

"That's pretty early," Corey said. "I don't think Ben and Ellen would let me ride my bike when it's dark out."

"We thought about that," Steve said. "You could spend Friday night at my house. Wendy will come by at three-thirty to pick us up."

"It might work, but I'll have to ask," Corey said. Steve wrote his telephone number on a piece of notebook paper for Corey. The three talked a little longer and then the car left. Corey squeezed the transmitter once as they were pulling away and Wendy beeped the horn. The boy and the bike headed home.

Corey got on the bus Monday morning knowing it was going to be a good day. It had been a while since he'd felt that way. He'd had good days—he was just never this sure about it. But he stopped being sure when Don got on the bus.

"Corey, what the heck were you thinking!" Don sounded mad. "Kim called me and said you were some kind of 'sicko.' Did you really lick her nose?"

Corey didn't know what to say. "I tried to kiss her, but I missed," he whispered angrily.

"What about the birds? Did you really sit and watch some birds…you know…"

"They were dancing! It's courtship! What's wrong with that?"

"Look, I'm sure this will all blow over so don't worry about it, but this is the kind of thing that gives a kid a reputation—and not a good one."

"I don't understand."

"Look, can't you just be like everyone else? Kiss girls on the lips, not the nose, and watch MTV, not some X-rated bird dance."

As Corey approached his locker, he could see a white sheet of paper taped to it. His optimism about the day diminished even farther as he got close enough to see what was written on it in large letters: "Corey Nelson is a nose licker." There was also a crude drawing of a head with an extremely large tongue licking the nose of another large head. Corey tore the sign down and crumpled it tightly in his hand.

While digging in his locker, he could feel the eyes of everyone on him. He quickly grabbed his books and headed straight to his first-hour class. As he entered the room, a voice from down the hall shouted, "Hey, crane lover!" Corey sat down and wished he were anywhere else.

Don came into the room carrying his books. "Sounds like you really got Kim ticked at you," he said.

"Not much I can do about that now."

"For starters, you could clean up your act! Stop hanging out in those woods and maybe come down to the mall once in a while." Corey didn't respond. "You can't expect to fit in when you keep acting so weird."

Corey had never given much thought to fitting in before. He just did what he wanted to do.

Math class was uneventful and was over too soon. Corey walked into his science class with his tray of slides and his folder of notes under his arms. "Looks like I'll need to get a slide projector in here—that is if you're actually planning to go through with it," Mr. Culex said, sounding annoyed.

"I'm ready. Let's get it over with."

Mr. Culex sent a student to the A.V. office in search of the projector. Minutes later, the principal came in with the projector and a video camera. Mr. Culex looked resentfully at Mrs. Danaus. "You don't mind if I tape this report," the principal said as a statement, not a question. "I heard it should be good."

"Ellen must have called Karen," Corey thought. The next few minutes were a blur. While Mr. Culex set up the projector and Mrs. Danaus adjusted the video camera, Corey stood in front of the room trying not to think of anything. He knew what he had to do. He would give his report exactly as he had rehearsed. He was confident about his material and his father's slides. He looked up—that was a mistake. A kid in the front row lifted a notebook, revealing a page in a way that only Corey could see. Corey saw the pencil drawing of a person dancing with a large bird. The caption said, "True love!" Corey began to perspire.

"If you're ready…" Mr. Culex said, as Mrs. Danaus flashed a hopeful grin. With index cards held firmly in his hand, Corey began.

> "The word 'prairie' comes from the French word 'perie,' which means grassland or grassy orchard. A prairie is an ecosystem made up mostly of grasses and is a direct result of the climate in which it's found. Prairies are usually found in places that are too dry for forests and too wet for deserts. Because the climate has changed many times over the last ten thousand years, the range of the North American prairie has also changed. During the warmer periods, prairie could be found at much higher latitudes than today. During cooler and wetter periods, trees gradually replaced prairies."

Corey briefly thought about the note on his locker and the crude drawing of the crane. His perspiring hands started to shake.

> "Three major types of prairie can be found in North America: shortgrass, tallgrass, and mixed. Shortgrass prairies are found in the dry rain-shadow of the Rockies. This land has been used as grazing land because the lack of water made it difficult to farm. The tallgrass prairies can be found farther east where there is more rain. Only one percent of the original tallgrass prairie is still around. Most of the tallgrass prairies were plowed for farms and

are now cornfields. The lack of trees and the deep soil created the perfect conditions for farming. Mixed prairies are found in the transition zone between the tallgrass and shortgrass prairies.

"Over four hundred million acres of North America was once prairie. It was the largest continual ecosystem in North America; now, it's broken into small pieces. Today, groups such as the Nature Conservancy have been working to save what remains. Two major prairie preserves are the Konza Prairie, in Kansas, which is part of the National Science Foundation's Long-term Ecological Research Program, and the Tallgrass Prairie Preserve in Oklahoma."

Corey dimmed the lights and turned on the projector. The darkened room allowed him to relax a bit. He continued his report, changing slides as he went.

"The stars of the prairie ecosystem are the grasses. Grasses such as big bluestem, little bluestem, and Indian grass can be found along most roadsides in Adams County. In the summer, needlegrass can be seen, with its peculiar form of seed dispersal. The barbs on the ends of these seeds would latch onto the fur of buffalo, only to drop off a few days later."

Corey passed a handful of needlegrass seed around from a bag Wendy had given him. These sharp-pointed seeds needed to be handled gently. The cries of pain began almost at once.

"Many prairie forbs can be found in Central Wisconsin. The Pasque Flower (Anemone patens) is one of the first flowers to bloom on the prairie. This plant was used to treat boils and sore eyes."

The rich colors of the flowers brought faint gasps and smiles from a few students. Similar to crowds watching a fireworks display, they quietly voiced their approval with each new slide. Corey allowed himself to feel good for a brief moment. The next slide was upside down. The word, "Looser!" rang anonymously from the back row. He gave passing thought to running out of the room but decided to continue.

"The lupine (Lupinus perennis) comes into bloom in May and is critically important to the life cycle of the Karner blue butterfly. If the lupine is eliminated, the Karner blue can't survive.

71

"Puccoon (Lithospermum canescens) blooms in May and is common on roadsides in Central Wisconsin. Some Native American tribes used the white seeds of the plant as sacred beads.

"Birds-foot violet (Viola pedata) blooms in spring and then seems to disappear. This was a source of vitamin C and also used to treat diarrhea.

"In midsummer, butterfly weed (Asclepias tuberosa) is the easiest plant to spot. Its bright orange flowers are an important feeding station for butterflies and its deep taproot helps it to survive during times of drought.

"Prairies are more than just plants; many animals also call the prairie home. Buffalo were an integral part of the prairie ecosystem. Everything about this animal helps it to survive in a prairie. It can go without water for a long time, its herding behavior helps to protect it from predators, and its teeth allow it to eat the abundant grasses.

"Around the year 1500, buffalo could be found in Central Wisconsin, although this was the edge of their range. The advance of the railroad was the beginning of the end for the buffalo. Market hunters used trains to carry buffalo meat to the restaurants in the East. In 1800 there were thirty million buffalo in North America. By 1870 there were twenty million and in 1889 there were only one thousand animals left. The plains Indians, whose survival depended on the buffalo, suffered greatly from their demise. Efforts to reverse this trend have started to bring the buffalo back. By 1950 there were 25,000 and in 1994 there were 200,000.

"There are no free-roaming buffalo in Wisconsin today, but there still are many prairie animals in our area. These include the white-tail deer, coyote, red fox, striped skunk, meadow vole, northern harrier, sandhill crane, upland sandpiper, bluebirds, and hundreds of insects. A prairie ecosystem is incredibly diverse.

"A prairie without fire will not stay a prairie long. Fire keeps prairies from turning into forests. Two hundred years ago, wildfires were common in Adams County, and, as a result, so were prairies. But as modern forest management and fire control gave us the pulp for paper and a safe place to live, they also began the slow process of changing an ecosystem. Animals that were dependent on the open grasslands could not compete in a wooded environment.

"The prairie remnants in Central Wisconsin are the last remaining part of what was a vast area of prairie and pine barrens. Many of the plants found here are rare. A few are endangered. Animals, such as the prairie chicken and the Karner blue butterfly, depend on the prairie ecosystem for their survival. A valuable and unique resource is in danger of being lost forever.

"In addition to saving prairie remnants, locally collected seeds could and should be replanted to establish new prairies. This is the process of restoration. Restorations take a great deal of work, but the end result can be a thing of beauty.

"People who understand ecosystems are more likely to value them. How can we ask people to save a rain forest far away if we can't save an endangered community in our own backyard? If we work directly to protect and raise awareness about this endangered ecosystem, years from now we will be able to return to see the results of our efforts.

"I'd like to end with a quote from Aldo Leopold: 'To keep every cog and wheel is the first precaution of intelligent tinkering.'"

Corey looked up at his audience. Mr. Culex was writing on a slip of paper and Mrs. Danaus was grinning. The students, all of whom by now had heard Kim's version of the ill-fated date, sat silent. It was as if Corey had just broken the first commandment of J.F.K. Junior High School: "Thou shalt not do more than absolutely necessary." Corey knew he had set things straight with Mr. Culex. He also knew that he'd just made himself even more of an outcast with his classmates.

"Nice work, Corey," Mrs. Danaus said as she left with the video camera. Mr. Culex handed Corey a slip of paper without saying a word.

Corey,

Nice work. Your research was very complete and it is clear you understand what you are talking about. In the future, you will need to slow down and try to look at your audience a little more.

You will receive an 'A' on this report. At this point I will consider you caught up for the quarter. Please try not to get behind again.

Mr. Culex

It wasn't the apology that Corey had been hoping for, but he would take what he could get. He folded the note and put it in his pocket.

The class period ended with yet another worksheet. As the students filed out, no one said a word to Corey. In fact, no one said much to him all day. He even ate lunch alone. Don said he had "something to do" and ate with more the popular kids. Having Don desert him hurt the most. It made him feel even more isolated, more unwelcome, and more alone. In PE, students doubled up in lockers in other rows rather than use a locker near Corey.

On the ride home, Don sat in the back of the bus until just before his stop, when he moved forward to Corey's seat and sat down. "Man, have you got people talking about you!"

"Yeah I know. I was there—remember?"

"That was quite a report you gave today."

"I'll go out on a limb and guess that the report didn't help things here."

"I'd say. Now they're calling you 'Professor Crane Lover'." Corey sank back in his seat. "Hey, relax. This is all going to blow over. Things will be back to normal soon."

"Does that mean you'll sit with me at lunch again?"

"Oh, that—sorry. I was being a jerk."

The bus stopped and Don got off. Corey stared out the window as the bus pulled away and a cold spring rain started to fall. It was looking as if he might have to choose between friends and the Barrens. Fitting in with the kids at school might help him to feel normal again. Being in the Barrens made him feel whole. Unfortunately, it didn't seem as if he could have both.

Two miles from home the bus passed a Chevy Blazer that was parked alongside the road. It was hard to miss the large antenna sticking out the roof. Corey didn't feel quite so alone. He would have to remember to ask if he could stay at Steve's house Friday night.

"How did it go?" Ellen asked as he walked in the door.

"I think I nailed it," Corey said. His false tone of excitement masked the stress he was feeling. "Too bad you couldn't have seen it."

"I wanted to wait until you and Ben were home," she said as she put the principal's videotape down on the table.

Corey just shook his head and laughed. "All I can say is I'm glad you're on my team."

"I am and don't you ever forget that." She gave him a gentle hug and said, "Take your things to your room. Before you ask, I don't want you riding down to the Barrens in the rain. That place will survive without you for a day."

After supper, the three sat in the living room and watched the video of the report. The sound quality was poor and the slides didn't show up well, but Ben and Ellen were proud of the performance. Corey, on the other hand, hated to see himself on videotape. He did look like a nerd. It was no wonder the kids picked on him so much.

"Nice work, Bud," Ben said. "What did Mr. Culex have to say about it?" When Corey showed him the note, he observed, "Well, could be worse. At least you won't have anymore problems at school."

Corey didn't want to explain that his problems at school were only just beginning.

"I ran into those two grad students again yesterday."

"The ones with the TV antenna in their car?" Ellen asked.

"Yeah. They're really cool. They were telling me about the prairie chicken booming grounds."

"I've heard of that," Ben said. "It was on that show on PBS."

"They want me to go sit in a blind with them next Saturday morning," Corey said, adding, "It would be really early."

Ellen's mother-radar was alerted. "How early?"

"We need to be in the blind by four-thirty."

"In the morning?" Ben exclaimed.

"If you get there any later you scare away the birds."

"You'll never get up that early!" Ellen said.

"That's why Steve asked if I could stay at his place Friday night."

Corey had been living with them for less than two weeks and Ellen was not about to let him spend the night at some college student's house. Especially a student she didn't know. Ellen had spent two years in college and knew too well what that could be like.

Ben understood what Ellen was thinking by the look on her face. He also knew that Corey needed to have opportunities like this, and that they would have to find a way to make it work. It took only a quick look, just a few seconds of silent eye contact, to reach a compromise. After twenty-five years of marriage, words weren't always necessary.

Ellen explained a counter-offer. "We can't let you spend the night at some college student's house. We haven't met the boy and don't know a thing about him." Corey looked disappointed. "However, if you can live with some minor changes in your plan, I think we can get you out to that blind."

Corey sat up and listened intensely.

Corey was sure that Steve and Wendy would laugh at him—many people had lately—but he'd ask anyway. He dialed the number and asked for Steve.

"Just a minute," was the reply. He could hear the shouts of "Hey, Steve, it's for you."

"Hello?"

"Steve, this is Corey Nelson—from the Barrens."

"Hi guy, how ya doing?"

"Okay. My foster parents won't let me stay at your house on Friday. They say I'm too young."

"I was afraid of that."

"But Ellen did say that you guys could stay here. She said it's closer and she'd even make breakfast. I know it sounds dweeby and I'll understand if you don't want to but it's the only way I..."

"Sounds great!"

"What?"

"Look, I haven't had a meal that didn't come out of a microwave in months. Is Ellen a good cook?"

"She's a great cook. Except for her meat loaf."

Steve laughed. "Wendy and I will be there around eight."

"Shouldn't you check it out with Wendy?"

"I've seen the stuff she eats—she'll be there."

"Cool."

"Take care kid. See you Friday night."

15
The Blind

The rest of the week saw no decrease in the harassment. Each day Corey would find a note either taped to his locker or on the back of the chair he sat in. Don sat with him at lunch, but it was clear he was uneasy about it. Mr. Culex continued to be as disinterested in Corey as he was in his job as a teacher.

Each day ended with a trip to the Barrens, where Corey could take some time to get away from thoughts of school. On Wednesday afternoon, a woodcock exploded from the brush just a few meters from where Corey was standing. Stepping on the well-camouflaged bird was the last thing on his mind, but the woodcock could think of nothing else. The blur of brown whistling wings flew deeper into the brush. A flash of boyish fear was quickly replaced with an adrenaline-charged sense of awe. How could he tell his classmates that this was more exciting to him than playing video games or hanging out at the mall?

In the lunchroom on Friday, Don turned to Corey and said, "I have a way you could clean up your image."

"Oh?"

"There's a party tonight at Jake's house."

"Like I'd ever get invited."

"No way—but if you walked in with me, they wouldn't tell you to leave. You'd just have to promise me you wouldn't act like a nerd or something." This would have been the wrong time for Corey to try to explain what his plans were for Friday night.

"Sounds good," Corey lied, "but I have to stay at home on Friday night."

"Sneak out."

"Can't. Ellen has a sister or something coming over to meet me." Corey lied again.

"Your loss. Jake already has a case of beer and his older brother says he could get us more."

This time Corey couldn't keep his feelings hidden with lies. With sudden anger he said, "Five months ago my parents were killed by a kid who'd had

77

too much beer. If I need to go to a beer party to be cool, then you'd better get used to eating lunch with a nerd."

"Sorry, I forgot." Don seemed a little shaken by what Corey had just said. The two said nothing more until the bell rang to end the lunch period. On the bus ride home, Don was still thinking about the exchange in the lunchroom. "I was a jerk this morning," he said without looking at Corey.

"Yeah. But you're also the only jerk in this school who will talk to me."

As the bus stopped to drop Don off, he turned to Corey and said, "Have fun meeting your foster aunt tonight." He would have expected anyone else to respond by saying "have fun too," but there was no way Corey was going to tell anyone to have fun at a beer party.

Corey simply said, "Thanks."

Wendy and Steve showed up at eight o'clock with sleeping bags and backpacks full of books. Wendy was also carrying her laptop computer. Corey took care of introductions and Ellen invited them to sit down at the dining room table.

"Would either of you like a cup of decaf?" Ellen said.

"Sure," Steve replied.

"Would you have any herbal tea?" Wendy asked.

Ben laughed quietly and said, "I think we do—somewhere."

Ellen brought out a chocolate cake and Steve's eyes grew wide. After finishing a piece in just a few seconds, he said, "Mrs. Raine, that cake was incredible. Corey said you were a good cook, but man, that was superb!"

"You're welcome to another piece as long as you promise to call me Ellen." After all of cake was gone, Ellen asked Corey to take Wendy's bags to the guest room. "Steve, I'm afraid you're stuck with the sofa."

"No problem. I once spent a week sleeping on a granite boulder in the Rockies." The rest of the evening was taken up with Ben and Steve swapping fishing stories, and Wendy studying for a test at the dining room table. The telephone rang.

"Corey, it's for you," Ellen said.

"Hello?"

"Hey, Corey, it's Don."

"Hi. I thought you were heading over to Jake's party."

"Yeah, well I guess this world needed one more nerd."

"Cool." Don's decision to skip the party made Corey feel a little dishonest. He decided to explain the real reason he had to stay home tonight. Don was silent on the other end of the telephone. Corey expected to be yelled at one more time for being a nature freak.

"Corey, you're a genius! You've got a good-looking college woman sleeping twenty feet from your bed and you got your foster mother to think it was her idea."

"Relax! We're just going to see some prairie chickens."

"That's even better yet! You two are going to slip off into the night and hide in a tent."

"Don, will you get your mind out of the gutter! We are going to see the prairie chickens. That's all."

"I know that and you know that. What's the big deal if we just leave out a few minor details."

"You're a strange kid, ya know that," Corey said with a laugh.

"Well never underestimate the power of a strange kid."

"If only you could use your powers for good instead of evil!" Corey said, trying to sound as much like Batman as he could. Don laughed. Corey laughed.

"Thanks for calling, Don."

"See ya in school, nerd. Things will get better." Only Don could make Corey feel good by calling him a nerd.

By 9:30, Corey had his clothes set out for the morning and was trying to sleep. Two thirty in the morning came quickly. Corey was awakened by the sound of a pan hitting the stove. Ellen was already cooking breakfast. Showered and dressed, he walked into the kitchen to find Steve busy eating pancakes, while Ellen carried over a plate of bacon.

"Hey, Corey," Steve said with a mouth full of food, "you sure were right. Ellen is a incredible cook." He turned to Ellen and said jokingly, "Can I come live with you?"

"Not a chance!" Ellen fired back with a smile. She walked over to Corey, gave him a hug, and said, "You're pretty ugly this time of the morning." Corey laughed and didn't say a word.

Wendy joined the early morning feast as Steve carried his plate to the sink, quickly filled it with hot soapy water, and began to wash the dishes.

"I'm surprised," Ellen said. "I didn't know college kids knew how to wash dishes anymore."

"My mama taught me well," he said with a fake Southern drawl.

"Just let me take care of the dishes and you can take your things out to the car."

Ten minutes later, Wendy, Steve, and Corey were driving down the road in the middle of the night. The blind was not in the Barrens. It was tucked away in a grassy forty-acre field behind a farmhouse a few miles from the Barrens. The game managers had been leasing this land from the farmer ever since they found that the prairie chickens used it for booming in the spring. The farmer still got to use it for grazing in the summer.

It took ten minutes to get to the place where they would park the car. Carrying the equipment the quarter mile down the dark path to the blind took another twenty minutes. The night was clear and cold. Wendy and Steve both held red flashlights. Steve explained that the red light would let them see where they were going without destroying their night vision. "What have you got in this pack?" Corey asked. "It weighs a ton!"

"Just stuff." Steve said. When they reached the blind, Corey watched in amazement as the equipment was unpacked. He saw a laptop computer, three pairs of binoculars, a portable radio receiver, two insulated jugs, and a large wool blanket.

The flashlights were shut off after the gear was tucked into the small blind. The starry night sky was incredible. Corey found the constellation Cygnus quickly and pointed it out to Wendy. "That's one of my favorites."

"Why's that?" Wendy asked.

"I don't know," Corey said, and he didn't. For a few minutes his mind was somewhere else. Just outside Mojave, California, was a place called Red Rock Canyon State Park. The stars were as bright as he had ever seen as he'd sat on the steep slope of a canyon wall with his parents. The plan was to stay awake until the moon rose over the rim of the canyon, but Corey had fallen asleep in his mother's arms watching Cygnus. She'd woken him up just in time to see the three-quarter moon make its stunning entrance. "Yeah, I guess I do know why it's my favorite," he said, but no one was close enough to hear him.

Corey thought about his parents. He had never thanked them for that trip. He had never taken the time to tell them how important they were to him. He knew that they knew, but he still wished he had said the words. He wouldn't make the same mistake with Ben and Ellen. He didn't know how long he would be staying with them, but he was going to be sure that he said everything that needed to be said. You just never know what could happen.

It was almost 3:30, so the three bird watchers crawled into the canvas blind. There was barely enough space for the three of them to sit on the plank that served as a bench. Through the glow of the red flashlights, Corey watched as the two graduate students got set for the morning performance. Steve was on his left. He had headphones connected to his portable receiver so he could hear if any of his birds were nearby. Once, just for fun, Corey squeezed his broken transmitter and Steve jumped.

On his right was Wendy. She had a spreadsheet up on the laptop and was entering some information about the time and location of this observation session. "I'll bet you use computers at school all the time," Wendy asked Corey in a quiet voice.

"Nope. I try to avoid them as much as possible."

"I would think you would be on the computers all day. Isn't that what kids do these days?"

"Most kids do, but not me. If you look carefully, the kids are usually playing video games. The stupid thing is they all have the cheat codes, so they can't lose. That's not my kind of fun."

"What's a cheat code?"

"It's really dumb. They play these games that require you to think in order to do well, but I guess these kids don't know how to think. They type in a 'secret code' that everyone knows and the game gives them a zillion extra points. These guys are stupid enough to think that they're beating the game. I'll bet that somewhere in Silicon Valley there is this programmer geek who's laughing at them right now."

"If you have the cheat codes so you can't lose, why bother playing?"

"Now you understand."

"But that's only a tiny part of what computers can do."

"I think it's all a waste of time."

"Don't give up on them so fast. They're revolutionizing the way we study ecosystems."

"Yeah, but I'm sure someone has got the cheat codes for that too."

Wendy pulled the lid down on her laptop and the blind went dark. Corey really didn't mind sitting this close to Wendy. She was perfect. She was smart and cute. Too bad she wasn't in junior high.

"If you're cold you can pull the blanket up that's under the bench," Wendy said. Adolescent thoughts quickly filled his head, but then left.

"I'm okay."

"Ellen packed some hot chocolate. You'd better have some now because when the show starts, you won't have time." Wendy lifted the lid on her laptop to provide a little light. Seeing the small computer used as a flashlight made Corey laugh. Finally, he'd found a practical use for computers. He poured a cup and offered it to Steve, who was listening to the headphones intently. He waved "Thank you" and went back to listening for his birds.

"We haven't heard from our birds for almost a week. He's really hoping one decides to show up this morning."

"What could have happened to them?"

"Coyote food."

"Ick."

"Yeah, well. They have to eat too."

Corey poured two more cups of hot chocolate and Wendy closed her two-thousand-dollar flashlight. Once again in the dark, Corey was trying to think of things to say.

Wendy beat him to it. "Do you like living with Ellen and Ben?"

"They're great."

"It must have been tough to lose your parents at your age." Usually he resented it when people said things like that. It was as if saying it would make him feel better. But something about the way Wendy asked the question made him comfortable enough to answer truthfully.

"It still hurts. Some days are worse than others. It's weird because some days I think about them and I just want to cry, but other times I think about them and it makes me feel good."

"Like before when you were looking at the stars?"

"How did you know?"

"My brother was killed by a drunk driver four years ago. I have good and bad days too."

"I'm sorry."

"Listen, if you ever need to sit and talk, just call me."

"Thanks, I may do that." They sat in silence for the next thirty minutes. The first hint that the prairie chickens were around would be the muffled clucking sound of the males as they established their territory on the booming ground. For now, there was only silence.

Corey was thinking about how quickly his image of Wendy had changed. An hour ago she was what Don would call a "babe." Corey would have loved to walk down the halls before school with her hand in his. Everyone would be jealous and Don would call him a "stud." But knowing that she was going through the same kind of pain as he was changed that. Empathy replaced more juvenile thoughts. Suddenly, this good-looking woman became simply a woman. She became someone who understood his grief. He felt guilty for the way he'd thought of her before and figured it would be something he should talk with Ben about.

The first sounds came when a lone male bird strutted its way onto the booming grounds. He made a brief motion with his wings that produced a loud click. The observers in the blind stopped whatever they were doing and waited for the next sound. They didn't have to wait long. Clicks were heard from several directions as the sun began to work its way to the horizon. They kept the small observation flap on the blind down for another ten minutes as the males began staking out their territory. Any unnecessary movement could spook the birds. Once the noise from the birds became almost constant, the flaps of the blind were lifted.

Corey looked out in amazement at the nine brown birds scurrying across the patch of short grass. With their wings spread open and bent down, they spun in circles and chased other males out of their territory. Corey was fascinated by the orange air sacs that the males inflated and then quickly deflated.

This created a reverberating, low-pitched booming sound that seemed to come from nowhere and everywhere at the same time.

Steve was watching while continuing to listen for the tagged birds. The intensity of the display increased dramatically when a hen walked onto the grounds. The level of violence seemed to increase also. Males began fighting to gain more territory and to hold on to what they had. The female walked from one displaying male to another, not staying for any longer than a minute. She finally selected an appropriate mate. How she made her selection was a mystery to Corey. Each bird's dancing skills looked the same to him. The coupling took less than a minute, then the hen left the booming grounds to build a nest. The male would have nothing to do with raising the young.

Corey thought about what had just happened. If he had been in the blind with kids from his class, the childish remarks and rude comments would have been hard to hear over the laughter. But sitting with two people who shared his interest in birds, the reaction was one of quiet fascination. He felt sad that there was no one his age he could share this experience with.

Steve looked up and whispered, "I think we have number three paying us a visit." He held his hands to the headset and said. "Number one is here also." Wendy gave him a "thumbs up" and a smile and then went back to entering data into her spreadsheet. Within a minute, two hens, both wearing small radio packs, strolled onto the booming grounds. The place went nuts! Every male was jumping, stomping, turning circles, and booming. One male jumped up on top of the canvas blind. Just inches from Corey's head, the football-sized bird was trying to gain the attention of the two new arrivals. The unusual perch must not have been to his liking because he quickly returned to the dance floor.

For more than an hour the display continued. It did not diminish until the sun climbed higher in the sky. By 6:30 the last prairie chicken had left the area. They waited a few minutes longer and stepped out of the blind into the cold morning air. None of the bird watchers noticed the bald eagle passing high over their heads.

"That was fantastic," Corey said.

"It was one of the best shows we've had all season," Wendy said.

Steve was less excited, saying only, "I wonder where chicken number two is hanging out?"

The three bird watchers packed up the gear and walked out. When they reached the car, Steve turned to Corey and asked, "Do you think Ben and Ellen would let you come to the university with us to turn in our data?"

Wendy added, "It's kind of exciting. All the teams from each of the blinds get together and report what they saw. They'll have sort of a brunch set up for us."

"Sounds like fun, but I don't think they'll let me go all the way into Stevens Point."

Steve said, "It can't hurt to ask."

"How did it go?" Ellen asked as they walked into the kitchen.

"It was a blast!" Corey said. "Any chance I could go with them to turn in our data?"

"You mean all the way into Stevens Point?"

"I can run him back out here when we're done."

The deal was made. Ellen let Corey go to the university as long as he was back by three o'clock. The half-hour drive was a non-stop, free-flowing discussion about anything and everything. Well, almost everything. Corey didn't want to explain to his new friends that he felt like an outcast at school. He didn't know how to say that the very thing that brought the three of them together would cause him to be even more isolated, if anyone at school were to find out.

The brick buildings on the Stevens Point campus looked new compared with the building Corey's father had worked in. There were fewer windows and smaller trees in comparison to the stately oaks at the Madison campus.

In the lobby of the College of Natural Resources, other prairie chicken counters were turning in their data sheets. Corey noticed a buffet table set up near the wall. After dropping off their data and making a quick trip past the steam table, the three settled down on a bench for a welcome, if informal, hot meal.

A woman with a note pad and a huge camera pulled up a chair and sat down beside them. "Hi, I'm Aster Laevis. I'm with the *Portage County Daily Times*. Do you mind if I ask you a few questions?"

"No problem," said Steve and Wendy at almost the same time.

Corey simply said, "Cool."

She took a few pictures and then asked, "I already have the background information I need about the prairie chickens. I also know why it's important to be out in the blinds on such a cold morning, but what I'd like to hear is why you chose to do this."

Wendy spoke first. "Steve and I are graduate students. We've spent most of the last year studying the greater prairie chicken."

Steve added, "If we can learn more about how it lives and what its habitat needs are, then we can do a better job of protecting it."

The reporter turned to Corey and asked, "Now I'm sure you're not in graduate school. What brings you here?"

Before he could speak Wendy jumped in. "Corey is incredible. He knows more about what goes on in a grassland ecosystem than most of the students in this building."

"So Corey, how did you get to be an expert at such a young age?" As Corey told his story, the reporter got excited. She could see the small story, which was to be buried somewhere in the back of the paper, getting bigger as he spoke. By the time Corey was done, she was sure she had a front-page feature.

Steve drove Corey home while Wendy headed to her part-time job as a waitress. "So Corey, how come you never talk about school?"

"I don't know. I just don't like it much."

"Must be tough to get dropped into a new school this late in the year."

"Yeah." Corey looked out the window.

"Have you made any friends at school? I'm guessing the girls are going nuts over you."

"Things are nuts, that's for sure, but not in a good way. I do have one friend—Don. The rest of kids are just stupid. They sit in front of the computer all day playing video games."

"Look on the bright side. There are only a few weeks left."

"Amen!"

Steve dropped Corey off at the farmhouse and headed back to town. Ellen was folding laundry as he walked into the kitchen. "You must be awfully tired right about now."

"No, it was fun. This reporter came and talked to us and she took my pict…"

Corey stopped in mid-sentence as Ellen started taking his undershorts out of a laundry basket and folding them. As his eyes grew wide Ellen shook her head. "Will you relax! How do you think your clothes get washed?"

Corey didn't say a word.

"Well, I'm glad you had a good time today. Now head upstairs and get cleaned up."

16

The News

At the start of Corey's third week of school, Don sat down next to Corey on the bus. "How was your hot date with the bird watcher?"

"It wasn't a date, and it was a blast! We saw all kinds of prairie chickens and I got to talk to a reporter. It was great."

"You spend a cold night snuggling up with a college woman and all you can talk about are some chickens?"

"They're prairie chickens."

"Sometimes I wonder about you."

"So what did YOU do Friday night when the rest of the school was at Jake's?"

"I sat around watching TV with my mom and her new boyfriend."

"So do you wish you would have gone to the party?"

"Not really."

The bus pulled into school to start what Corey had hoped would be an uneventful day. The first two hours were certainly boring enough. Third hour in the library changed all of that when Ms. Asio dropped a copy of the *Wisconsin Sentinel Gazette* on the table in front of him. "Central Wisconsin Youth Works to Save Threatened Birds," was written across the top of section two in big letters, along with a picture of Corey sitting next to Wendy and Steve.

"It looks like the article was even picked up by the wire services," said Ms. Asio. "It says that you're an expert on grassland birds."

"No, I'm not. I just think they're cool."

"Well I think this article is cool."

"I guess." Corey didn't admit that he thought it was cool too. Any other place or time and he'd be jumping on the furniture with joy, but at this school, that article was bad news. The only good thing was that no one ever read the newspaper.

"Here, why don't you take this extra copy home. I'm sure your foster parents would love to see it."

"Thanks Ms. Asio." Corey hid the article in his folder. He would show Ben and Ellen, but no one else.

Walking to lunch, Corey noticed a crowd of students gathering around the office window looking at something that had just been posted. As he got closer, he saw the newspaper article, laminated and taped to the inside of the glass. He knew he was in trouble now.

In the lunchroom there were a few more stares than usual, and in the hallway he heard his name mentioned a few more times than was commonplace, but there were no major incidents—until seventh hour.

Corey was almost finished getting dressed when it happened. Someone threw a towel over his head from behind and pulled it back hard. This not only acted as a blindfold, but also served to pull him to the ground. The first fist hit his head before he could struggle to get free from the blindfold. Reeling from the pain, he curled up on the floor as the next six blows found his head. A kick to the back made a loud thud, and the unknown attackers ran off. The next sound Corey heard was the voice of Mr. Taxidea. "Hey Corey, what happened?"

As Corey tried to explain what had happened, he found the note that was taped to his back. It read, "Nice Article Prairie Fairy." He had reached his limit. Corey put his head in his hands and cried.

Less than thirty minutes later, he sat in the passenger seat of Ellen's car heading home. "How long has this been going on?" she asked.

"A while, I guess, but I've always been able to handle it."

"You should have talked to us about it."

"I know, but I thought it was getting better."

"Apparently it wasn't. I'll talk with Karen and we'll get this all straightened out."

"I'm not going back."

"Oh yes you are."

"What's the use, I'll never fit in there."

"What will you prove by not going back?"

Corey didn't answer. He just looked out the window at the potato fields.

"Could you drop me off at the Barrens and let me walk home?"

Ellen understood what he was really asking for. He needed some time alone to work this out. She knew very well what that was like. She also knew that she'd needed almost eight years to do the same thing.

"Can you be home in an hour?"

"I guess."

Ellen dropped Corey off at the large wooden sign. She looked around at the openness of the area and had to admit to herself that she didn't understand his attachment to this place. But he liked being here and that was good enough.

It was always windy in the Barrens, but today the wind was stronger than usual. The wind rushing past his ears kept Corey from hearing anything but a constant muffed roar. He would hear no cranes today, but he didn't mind. It was a warm spring day and he was where he wanted to be—anywhere but at school.

He knew that Ellen and Ben would insist he return to school tomorrow. There would be no way to avoid that. He'd heard Mrs. Danaus tell Ellen that the four kids who attacked him would be out of school for three days, and when they returned, they would be under threat of expulsion if there was any more trouble. But that was only a small part of the problem. Once again he felt like an outsider just because he was different.

Corey lay down on the mat of dead grass and watched the clouds blow by. He focused on one cloud bank in particular and tried to block everything else out of his mind. The wind was getting stronger as he continued to concentrate on the rising cumulus clouds. If this were any other time, he would have noticed that the first spring thunderstorm was building. But he was not think-ing about storms right now. He was trying not to think about anything.

Corey began to feel lightheaded so he closed his eyes. When he reopened them, the dizziness was still there, but it was different somehow. Instead of watching the clouds from the grassy field, he felt almost as if he were in them. He could feel himself being pulled up with the rising air currents and turning circles through the clouds. He felt somehow free from the weight of gravity. He saw—or imagined he saw—the Barrens as if he were high above it in a plane. With a clarity he had never before experienced, he could see the stands of oaks and the deer trails. He could see the large wooden sign and the road that led to his house. Throughout this imagined flight he felt unusually secure—a sense of security he hadn't felt for months.

He closed and reopened his eyes once more and the feeling was gone. The wind was calmer and his head felt better. He sat up and gazed at the line of clouds that continued to build and saw a speck turning circles in the sky. He didn't have to study it long to figure out what it was. He already knew. It was a bald eagle.

Corey sat for a few minutes to clear his head before starting his walk home. He knew he would have to go to school tomorrow, so he would just have to find a way to deal with it. Simply put, he had to choose between fitting in at school or being the kind of kid he wanted to be. It really wasn't a choice, it was more of a realization. He was who he was, and if the kids at school didn't like it, too bad. With his spirits lifted by having sorted out the issue and by that strange dream, he felt he could now face whatever the last weeks of the school year had to throw at him.

"Before you say a word," Corey said to Ellen as he walked in the door, "I'm going to school tomorrow. I've decided that I can't let a few jerks try to tell me how to live."

"You sure are a stubborn kid. That's one of the things I love about you."

Corey smiled. "When will Ben be home?"

"He called this morning from Milwaukee. He said he should be home by five, but the storms may slow traffic a bit. Why don't you go get cleaned up?"

A heavy spring rain was falling outside. Corey sat at the table after dinner as Ben and Ellen drank coffee. "Even if the kids at school don't think the newspaper article was impressive, we certainly do," Ben said. He lifted a small wrapped package from the floor and set it on the table in front of Corey. "We wanted to get you something to celebrate."

Corey couldn't think of anything to say. He just looked at the package. "Thanks," he finally said.

"Well, open it," Ellen prodded. Corey slowly pulled the paper away from the box, revealing a small cassette player and a pair of headphones.

"It's been a while since I've picked out a gift for a teenager. I think I goofed," Ben said, looking disappointed in himself. "It just dawned on me that you don't have any tapes to listen to."

"I have one," Corey said. "In fact, it was last thing my father ever gave me. This is perfect, thank you."

A smile returned to Ben's face.

"Why don't you take it upstairs and try it out," Ellen said. "But I don't want you listening to it while you do your homework. Okay?"

"Sure." Corey stood and turned back to face Ben and Ellen. With both hands tightly gripping the back of a kitchen chair, he said slowly, choosing his words carefully, "It seems like you're the only people who really like being around me. But..." Corey swallowed hard, "what if they send me someplace else and the people aren't like you?" It was clear by the look on his face that this was something he had been thinking about for a while.

Ellen was shaken by the question. She had gotten so used to his living here that she had not considered his ever leaving. "No one is taking you away, so just relax," she said.

"I guess," Corey said, not sounding convinced. He headed upstairs.

Ellen was not convinced either.

"That's the second time he's brought that up," Ben said, as he reached for Ellen's hand.

"It makes no sense worrying. There's nothing we can do about it anyway."

"Yes, there is."

Lying on his bed, Corey looked at the last tape his father had given him. Neatly printed on the side of the tape case were the words, "Another Challenge." It had been a game between them. He would string together a collection of rock tunes and Corey would try to guess what they had in common. The first tape his father made was easy; it was all songs about rain. The next tape was more difficult. It was a collection of songs that had Jackson Browne singing somewhere in the background. It had taken Corey a month to figure the meaning. He held the last tape, knowing only that it contained a collection of songs his father had wanted him to listen to and understand. He would never know if he'd solved the challenge.

He remembered how his father would try to explain the meaning of the lyrics to songs. Corey understood most of them. His mother's Bee Gee albums were another thing altogether. He would spend hours arguing with his father about what the lyrics meant. That's one of the things he missed—arguing. Not fighting. Not yelling. Just friendly arguing. Sometimes it went on for days. Sometimes his father would say things he didn't mean just to get an argument started. It was one of the few times when Corey felt that an adult respected him. He wasn't "too young to understand." But those days were gone. His father's albums, along with everything else that had been in the apartment, were in a storage locker in Madison. He would listen to this tape, but there would be no one to argue with.

Corey put the headphones on and pressed play. He turned the light off and hit the bed as the first guitar riff of a Peter Gabriel song, titled *Solsbury Hill*, began. He resolved to concentrate extra hard to understand the lyrics.

Corey was overwhelmed by the lyrics. With each song he listened to, he was carried deeper and deeper into his hidden memories of his father. Corey fell asleep wishing he could be near him again.

Ben and Ellen slept through the crashes of thunder, but were wakened by a muffled scream. "I'll go," said Ben. Corey's door was open and his light was on as Ben walked in. "You okay Bud?"

"Yeah—I just don't like storms."

"Let's go down and see what's on TV," Ben said.

"Good idea."

The two settled in on the sofa. No words were spoken—none were needed. Corey moved so he could rest his head on Ben's shoulder. Within minutes they were both asleep with the TV still on. Five o'clock in the morning found the TV off and a comforter over the two of them.

17
The Next Day

The storms from the night before had passed, leaving a cloud bank that was tinted deep purple as the morning sun lit the sky. Corey stared at the brightening horizon as he waited for the bus. Yesterday's locker room attack left no marks that others could see. Using two mirrors and a great deal of stretching, he did manage to get a look at the large bruise on his back. The lasting scars were on the inside. He would not admit it to Ellen, but he was afraid to get on the bus. With the possible exception of Don, no one at school seemed to think it unusual to beat someone up just because they were different.

The first part of the ride would be the worst. The bus would start out nearly empty but would fill quickly. With each stop more students would get on, walk past Corey, and talk to each other just loud enough to let him hear. At least when Don got on the bus, he would have someone to talk to, and he wouldn't have to hear the others.

The bus slowed at the Raines driveway and the driver switched on the red flashing lights. Corey was more nervous now than he'd been on the first day of school. With the screeching of brakes, the bus came to a stop and the door opened. Corey took a deep breath and stepped up and into the bus. He didn't see Ellen at the window of the farmhouse peeking from behind the curtain.

"Hey nerd! Want a donut?"

"Don! What are you doing here?"

"I guess I just wanted to see what the boonies looked like this early in the morning."

Corey took the seat next to Don and stuffed a jelly donut in his mouth. Don had to have gotten up at least an hour earlier than usual to be on the bus already.

"You didn't have to do this, you know."

"I know."

"But I'm glad you did."

"I know." Don reached in his pack and handed him a folded piece of paper in the shape of a triangle. "Here, it's from Kim."

"Not again!"

"Just read it." Corey unfolded the note and began to read.

Corey,

I'm sorry about what happened to you in school today. Those guys are jerks and I'm glad they got kicked out of school for a while. You're still the weirdest boy I've ever known, but that's no reason for someone to beat you up. I was thinking that maybe we could be just friends.

Kim

Corey folded the note and put it in his backpack. "You know I'm never gonna fit in, don't you?"

"Why do I get the feeling that you don't even plan to try?"

"Nope—not going change a thing."

"You're a stubborn little nerd, aren't you?"

"Deal with it!" Corey grabbed another donut.

"I never told you, but I saw you out there."

"Out where?"

"Out in that chicken place."

"It's called the Barrens."

"Whatever." Don took a bite of his donut. "My mom dragged me to Plainfield to see her boyfriend's pool tournament and we took a shortcut. At least it would have been a shortcut if we hadn't gotten lost. Anyway, we ended up going past the Barrens. I saw this bike leaning up against a big wooden sign, and then saw you out in the middle of a big field." He turned to face Corey. "You were just sitting there." His voice made it clear that he didn't understand why anyone would do that. "It was almost like you were in church or something."

"I like being out there—I can't explain it. I'd like to think that, at least with you, I wouldn't have to try."

"Look, you go ahead and be as weird as you want. The way I figure it, everybody's weird in one way or another. You're just stupid enough to let people know about it."

"Thanks—I think."

The bus pulled up to the school and Corey reluctantly got out of his seat and headed inside. The halls were as crowded as ever. Kids were digging in their lockers, teachers were standing in the hall drinking coffee, and the P.A. was making announcements that everyone ignored. In other words, it was a normal morning.

94

Corey dumped his jacket in his locker, grabbed his books, and quickly went to his math classroom. He had expected the harassment from yesterday to continue, but it didn't. No one seemed to remember that just eighteen hours earlier, he had gotten beat up for being different. As other students came into the classroom they looked at Corey, but no one teased him. A few even said "Hi."

"Hey, nerd, what are you doing in here?" It was Don. "We've got six minutes before class starts. Let's walk the halls."

"It's probably better if I just stay here."

"Get your butt out of that chair and let's go." As Corey walked down the hall with Don, no one noticed him. Kim smiled and said "Hi," but everyone else found him as interesting as the paint on the wall. Corey was relieved. At this point, being ignored was a good thing. The warning bell rang and they headed to their first-hour class. Math and science passed without incident.

Ms. Asio was putting up a bulletin board as Corey walked into the library third hour. She was standing on a small stool adjusting letters across the top that spelled out "The Land Down Under." "Hi Corey, how are you feeling?"

"I'm okay."

"Good. Could you give me a hand with this?"

"I guess."

"If you hand me those pictures, I'll staple them up."

"Cool pictures. Did you take 'em?"

"Thanks. They're from my trip to Australia last summer."

"What's this one?" Corey held up a picture of a large, red-tinted hill completely devoid of vegetation.

"That's Ayers Rock. It was one of my favorite places on the whole trip."

"Looks like a neat place, but what is it?"

"Ayers Rock is in the Uluru National Park, which is in the Northern Territory of Australia. Uluru is the Aboriginal name for it. Geologically, it was formed about five hundred fifty million years ago in the Precambrian era. Over time, erosion sculpted the rock into the shape you see here.

"For the Anangu, the aboriginal people of Central Australia, it's a spiritual place," she continued, "It's important for the 'Dreamtime' or '*Tjukurpa*'."

"What's that?"

"*Tjukurpa* is a religious philosophy. It's how the Anangu answer questions about the meaning of life."

Corey carefully spun the large globe next to the bulletin board and said, "That sounds a little strange."

"Not really, if you think about it. People all over the world have places that are spiritually important to them, places they go when they're looking for answers. If you were to walk into any church in this town, I'll bet you'd find someone sitting quietly, just thinking. They could sit anywhere, but they choose to sit in church. The point is, it's the place that they find important. Have you ever heard of Mecca or Mount Fuji?"

"Yeah."

"Well, if you were to do a little research, you'd find hundreds of places like that, all around the world, that are spiritually important to one culture or another."

Corey handed Ms. Asio the last of the pictures. "I have an aunt who goes to Graceland every year. Is that the same thing?"

"On a personal level, I guess it is. I think people have more of a connection to certain places than they are willing to admit. I have a good friend who goes to Door County almost every weekend. She sits on the same rock and stares out at Lake Michigan. It's her own version of Ayers Rock."

"It still seems a little weird to me."

"Tell you what, I'll pull some books that might do a better job of explaining it. You could always do an Internet search. I'm sure there's a ton of stuff on the computer."

"No way. I can't stand to use those stupid things."

Ms. Asio just laughed and shook her head.

The rest of the day was boring. Corey liked it that way. While he was sitting in homeroom, Ms. Asio walked in with an armful of books. She went straight to Corey's desk and said, "We're shutting down the library for the year in a few weeks, so you'd better get to work." Corey smiled. Not only did he have the books he wanted, but also the library was closing. If the horned larks were the first sign of spring, the library closing for inventory was the first sign of summer vacation.

18
Fire

Corey spent the rest of the week splitting his free time between reading and walking in the Barrens. The wildlife managers at the Barrens were busy plowing firebreaks. These six-foot wide strips of bare soil would help keep planned fires under control. Each year they selected parts of the Barrens for burning to keep the trees short and the grasses robust. Prairie plants had such long roots that they could survive the fires. The weeds and most of the trees could not. The result was a landscape that looked much as it did three hundred years ago. Because only part of the area was burned each year, at any one time there was habitat in different stages of succession. This diversity kept the whole ecosystem healthy. The timing of the burn itself depended on the weather. It was important to have just the right amount of wind and a proper relative humidity. The goal was to get a complete burn without it getting out of control. Two days in a row the fire crew was all set to start, but the wind picked up and they were forced to abandon their plans for the day.

Corey walked through an area that was ringed by a firebreak. He knew this area would be blackened by fire any day now, only to be lush and green a few weeks later. The nutrients locked up in the plant tops that burned would feed the roots of the plants that survived. He watched a deer mouse scurry through the grass in front of him. Although he knew that the mouse would be safe underground during the fire, he was still bothered by the thought that some animals would not survive. His knowledge of the ecosystem told him it was good for the grassland, but his emotions told him otherwise.

Corey saw two large birds fly swiftly by. He watched the birds with amazement. The harriers were flying too fast, and changing direction too often, to watch with the binoculars. Most days they could be found flying low to the ground, hoping to surprise a field mouse that had made the mistake of being caught out in the open. Today was different. The birds were not gliding silently near the ground. They were climbing, diving, turning circles, and climbing again. The untrained eye would think that these birds were sick, or drunk.

Corey knew better. This was courtship—a time when logic is lost and hormones take over. All done to show the rest of the harriers in the area that this was their territory and that they were a pair.

Corey had to laugh. He couldn't help but think about the "couples" in school. Like the harriers, they too were controlled by something other than reason. Walking hand in hand down the hall, looking straight ahead, never at each other, one walks the other to class. Like the harriers, they performed their ritual as a way of announcing to the rest of the school that they were a couple.

Friday came quickly. Corey returned the pile of books to the library before heading to math class. Minutes after class started, the P.A. system interrupted Mrs. Burns as she was asking for last night's homework.

"Could you send Corey Nelson to the office."

"Sure thing," Mrs. Burns said to the wall.

"Tell him to bring his jacket, he's going home." Corey began to get scared. There were only a few reasons that he would be going home and none of them were good. His heart began to race as he fumbled with his locker combination. He threw some books in his backpack, grabbed his coat, and closed his locker a little too loudly. Was Ellen sick? Did Ben get in an accident with his truck? Was he being sent away?

Ellen was standing in the office as he came in. Her face gave no clue as to what was up. "You'll have to sign out, Corey," said the woman behind the desk. Next to where he signed his name was a space labeled, "Reason for Leaving."

"What do I put down for a reason?"

Ellen quickly said, "You're needed at home."

As soon as they left the building, Corey turned to Ellen and asked, "Is Ben all right?"

"Ben's fine. Just relax."

"Am I being sent away?"

Ellen stopped, turned to Corey, and put her hand on his cheek. "That's not going happen—you got it? We pulled you out of school today because we thought it was important. You'll understand soon enough." Minutes later they were in the car heading home.

Corey saw the column of smoke from five miles away. "They're burning the Barrens!" he shouted. As they got closer to home, the smell of the burning grass filled the car. Instead of turning toward the house, Ellen headed straight to the Barrens. Corey saw Wendy's Blazer parked next to the pale-green fire trucks from the Department of Natural Resources. Steve was at Corey's window before Ellen had the car shut off.

"Hey kid, glad you could make it."

"What?"

Ellen said, "He's a little in the dark. You might want to explain it to him."

"Okay," Steve said. "I pulled a few strings and got the okay to have you out here for the burn. Seems the wildlife managers liked what you said in that newspaper article. There are a few rules though. You'll have to stay with me at all times, and if the wind picks up, we're out of here. Got it?"

"Cool!"

"I have a rule also," Ellen said. "You aren't going anywhere in your school clothes." Ellen handed him a duffel bag. "You can either change on the other side of that truck, or we can go home quickly and you can change there." Not wanting to miss a thing, Corey grabbed the bag and walked behind the fire truck. He quickly changed and returned, tossing the bag into Ellen's car. She beeped the horn and waved as she drove away.

"She's a cool lady," Steve said.

"Yeah." Corey smiled. "Where's Wendy?"

"She's out on a four-wheeler with the portable receiver. We have our birds in this area, so we need to know how they react to the fire."

Corey and Steve got a good view of the whole operation by standing on the roof of Wendy's car. The backfires were started on the downwind side. People wearing large metal backpacks that had a pumping spray wand attached kept these fires from jumping the firebreak. The fire crew called them "piss buckets," and after Corey saw how they worked, he understood why.

As the backfires slowly burned into the wind, they used up any fuel that was on the ground. This had the beneficial effect of widening the firebreak, making it safe to start the primary fire. Using torches that dripped burning fuel, the crew started a line of fire on the upwind side. With the help of the wind, the fire raced across the area. Orange and yellow flames reached thirty feet into the air, and gray clouds of sweet-smelling smoke drifted everywhere. A tornado-like funnel formed as the burning grasses created their own wind. The fire sounded like the roar of jet engines. Corey was spellbound.

The show lasted about two hours. As the primary fire reached the backfire, the flames died down and only smoke could be seen. "Time to go to work," Steve said to Corey as he jumped down from the roof. Corey jumped down and followed Steve.

"What's up?"

"We get to help with the mop up. We'll walk around and spray water on any stumps that are smoldering, which should keep the fire from starting again after everyone leaves." Steve lifted a metal backpack and helped Corey adjust the straps. It was much heavier than Corey had expected, but he was not about to complain. As was the case with most of the backpacks, Corey's had leaks that quickly soaked the back of his sweatshirt.

For the next hour-and-a-half, Corey walked from one smoldering clump to another spraying streams of cold water. With each clump he visited, ash-filled steam lifted into the air and covered him completely. He saw how dirty the rest of the crew was and hoped he looked at least as bad. As the work continued, the backpack became lighter. By 2:00 the fire was out and the crew was eating a very late lunch.

"How are you holding up?" Steve asked.

"I'm beat, but I'm having a blast!"

"Glad to hear it. But I do have some bad news for you."

"What's that?"

"You look awful, and frankly, you stink!" Steve laughed as Corey threw a banana peel at him.

"You two look like you're having too much fun." It was Wendy.

"Hey Wendy," Corey said.

"How did our children do?" Steve asked.

"Both number one and number three flew off at the first sign of fire. Still haven't heard from number two."

"I'll take two out of three," Steve said.

Wendy spread old bed sheets out on the seats of her car to protect them from dirty clothes. A few members of the fire crew came over to say good-bye. "You handled yourself pretty well out there, kid," said a man with the name "Mike" printed on his jacket.

"Thanks," Corey said as he got into the car.

In minutes, they arrived at the farm, and Corey invited them in for a soda. "No thanks," Wendy said. "Steve needs a shower really bad."

"No," said Steve. "I need a really good shower."

"So do I!" Corey said. "Thanks for everything."

"No problem kid," Steve said. "We'll be gone for a few weeks so you take care of yourself, okay?"

"Sure."

"We'll touch base with you when we get back."

"Don't worry about that," Corey said as he gave the transmitter in his pocket a squeeze. "I know how to get a hold of you." Steve laughed as the receiver in the truck started to beep.

Corey walked to the house as the car pulled away. He saw a note taped to the door. Corey had learned to hate notes.

Don't even think of coming into this house with those clothes on.
Please leave them in the barn.

In the barn, Corey found his robe and another note telling him to go straight to the shower. He wondered aloud if there would be yet another note in the bathroom.

After quickly changing into his robe, Corey ran barefoot to the house. "Hi Ellen, I'm home!" he yelled as he walked in the door. Ellen had her head tucked under the sink and was adjusting a rusty pipe wrench.

"Did you have a good time?" Ellen's voice was muffled by the cabinet and gained a strange echo.

"It was great! Thanks."

Ellen crawled out from under the sink and wiped something black off the wrench. "Tell me all about it after you get cleaned up."

Corey went straight to the bathroom and indeed, found yet another note taped to the glass. This one told him to bring his clothes from the barn to the basement to be washed. The note ended with "love ya!"

The shower was great. The warm water felt much better than the wet sweatshirt he'd worn all morning. He was amazed at how black the soapsuds were as the water flowed down the drain. Ten minutes into his shower the water suddenly went cold. Ellen was running a load of whites and he was now competing for the limited hot water. He quickly dried off and reached for his robe. The smell of smoke on the robe made it unwearable, so once again, he had to make a dash to his room in a towel. Corey put on clean clothes, lay down on his bed, and immediately fell asleep.

19
Duck Pond

The end of the school year was uneventful. The kids who had beaten up Corey returned but left him alone. Don hung out with Corey as much as he could before he left to live with his father for the month of June.

Since school was out, Corey had more time to explore the Barrens. On warmer days he would check out his favorite duck pond. The wildlife managers dug a few of these throughout the Barrens to provide nesting sites for ducks and a water source for other animals. This one provided one more benefit: a place to swim. Located a mile and a half from the nearest road, the pond covered almost three acres. This was much larger than the other ponds he knew about. It was also deeper.

Corey didn't often swim in the pond because doing so chased the animals away, and Corey liked to see the animals most of all. No matter how slowly and calmly he tried approaching the pond, they knew he was there. The chorus frogs would stop singing and the tree swallows would find another place to hunt insects. Corey knew that if he kept absolutely still for twenty minutes, the show would start again. The tree swallows would again skim the surface of the water for a drink and the chorus frogs would start their high-pitched calls. Sometimes a bullfrog would add a bass line to the tune. Every now and then a deer would come down for a quick drink.

In the middle of the pond he could not touch bottom, even on his deepest dives into the dark brown water. He liked not touching bottom. The bottom was mucky. The bottom was slippery. The bottom was gross. It bothered Corey that touching the bottom bothered him. He felt he was acting like the kids at school, and they were stupid. He knew what the muck was. It was nothing more than the leaves of grasses and water plants that were breaking down, decomposing, on the bottom of the pond. He knew it was important to the health of the pond community. Nutrients locked in the leaves of the plants were being made available to other parts of the ecosystem. It was like the story, "Odyssey," that his mom read to him from *A Sand County Almanac*. He would never tell anyone he didn't like the feel of the dark wet muck on his feet. He really didn't like to tell anyone much about himself at all. They wouldn't understand.

It had been hot for a week. Today it would hit 95 degrees by the middle of the afternoon. Corey knew that the heat came from a high-pressure system parked over the state. Dry, hot air was pouring in from the desert southwest. The sky was cloudless and it had not rained in days. People in town were spending every waking minute putting water on lawns and gardens.

"People are stupid," Corey muttered. "They take plants that are not adapted to this climate and plant them in sandy soil that can't hold any water. Then they are rewarded with well-watered weeds and a lawn that needs to be cut every week. How dumb!"

Corey scanned the open land surrounding him. It wasn't really prairie; it was more of a scrubland. Many years ago, wildfires would have passed through here just often enough to keep most of the trees out. Only oaks survived. Filling the spaces between the oaks, grew deep-rooted prairie plants. These plants didn't need watering; they were doing just fine. Their deep roots let them take advantage of whatever rain happened to fall.

After checking the sandy edge of the pond for new animal tracks, Corey decided it was hot enough for a swim. The first time he swam here he was very self-conscious. Leaving his clothes on far enough from the pond to stay dry, he ran into the cool water. As far as swimming "au naturel," Corey rationalized that if someone wanted to see his naked butt so badly as to sneak a mile and half through the grass on a hot and humid day, there was nothing he could do about it.

It took him only a few minutes to relax enough to enjoy the swim. The water at the surface was as warm as bath water. Just eight inches below the surface, groundwater was keeping the temperature near 70 degrees. The trick was to kick only enough to mix the water to a comfortable temperature.

Corey relaxed and tried to forget about everything. But he also forgot about the crop dusters.

To get the correct angle of attack for spraying insecticides on the potato field adjacent to this part of the Barrens, a pilot had to pass over the pond at about one hundred fifty feet. The roar of the Piper Pawnee's engine came on quickly, and the sound was made even louder by the sudden rush of adrenaline Corey felt as he dove deep into the pond to hide. He hit the muck. Corey hated the muck.

The next pass took the small, yellow plane a little to the east of the pond. With each subsequent pass, the plane moved even farther away. Corey wondered if he had been caught. "Did the pilot see me in the pond?" Corey wondered. "If so, what exactly did he see?" Corey got dressed and started the long walk back to his bike.

As he hit the main road, he heard the plane engine again. The plane was much higher this time, probably heading home to refuel and reload the spray tanks. Corey kept telling himself that he had not been seen. What were the chances that the pilot was looking at that very spot, at that very instant? Corey smiled and relaxed. It was summer and he was not in school. It was at that moment that he noticed the plane again. It had changed course to fly directly over him, dipping the wings as he passed. Corey stopped smiling and was no longer relaxed.

It rained heavily through the night and Corey did not sleep well. His thoughts drifted from his parents, to Ellen and Ben, to that stupid crop duster, and to the Barrens. He didn't understand why, but he liked being in the Barrens. No, it was more than just liking the place. He somehow needed to be there. Maybe it was like Ayers Rock or Graceland.

The sun was coming up and Corey could hear Ellen in the kitchen. The radio was on too loud, as usual, and tuned to the public radio station. "Your breakfast is getting cold," Ellen called up the stairs.

"Be down in a minute." Corey never liked getting up early, but these days being awake was easier than trying to sleep. Awake he could always find other things to think about. Sleeping, or at least trying to sleep, gave him too much time to think about his parents.

"Morning, Corey," Ellen said calmly. Corey liked the way she didn't ask too many questions. In fact, she and Ben seemed to be the only ones who didn't. Everyone else wanted to know what he was feeling, wanted to get inside his head, wanted to pry.

As Corey sat down to a plate of pancakes, the woman on the radio was running down the list of topics for the morning. "Coming up at eight, Eric and his guest will discuss possible changes in the income tax code." Corey rolled his eyes. "At eleven, Alice is in with Dr. Bill Whitehorse from the University of Wisconsin Extension office to talk about the role of wildflowers in a grassland ecosystem." Corey snapped his head so fast it surprised even Ellen, who was paging through a catalog of courses offered by a community college. Finally, something on public radio that real people could listen to.

It was a little after six. If he did his chores quickly, he would still be able to spend some time in the Barrens and make it back by eleven to hear the radio show. Corey straightened up his room, fed Ponch, filled the birdbath, and mowed the patch of lawn he'd missed the day before.

A quick pass through the garden and Corey came up with a bowl of small potatoes for supper. The other day, he hadn't understood why anyone would dig them up when they were so small. Then he'd tasted them. About the size of a golf ball, they seemed to melt in his mouth. Of course, it helped to cover them in real butter. His mother had always used some fat-free, tasteless, butter-like, spread that turned to water when it melted. Looking down at the unwashed potatoes reminded Corey of yesterday, of crop dusters, and of how his swim was cut short by a fool in a plane.

The path into the pond took Corey past some familiar sites. The area that had been burned in May was already green. The spiderworts were in full bloom. The lupine had lost their flowers weeks ago and now had seed pods that looked like peas. His father had explained that lupine and peas were both legumes, which meant they could take nitrogen out of the air and change it into a form that plants could use. The short clumps of pale green grass were big bluestem. Corey remembered how the big bluestem had towered over his head on a September field trip with his father. "If I'm still here in September…" Corey stopped the thought as quickly as it started.

Standing on the edge of the duck pond, Corey thought about the crop duster and laughed. Leaving a pile of clothes on the shore, he slowly walked across the mucky pond bottom until it was deep enough for swimming. Corey hated muck.

His swimming skills definitely came from his mother. His father could swim, more or less, but he looked like he was attacking the water more than swimming through it. His mother was graceful, almost otter-like, in the water. She had taught Corey to swim while at the biological field station on Pigeon Lake, where his father was an instructor for a summer course. In the heart of Chequamegon National Forest, this was a perfect place for a family to spend time together.

Corey was a strong swimmer, but mostly he just liked to float, making as few waves as possible which gave him a different view of the pond. The water striders skimmed by just inches from his chin like spiders, using the surface tension of the water to keep them afloat. Half-inch beetles, called water boatmen, rowed just below the surface, passing their time feasting on algae. The frogs, silenced by Corey's swimming, started calling again, and a yellow swallow-tailed butterfly flew near the pond's edge. A squadron of dragonflies patrolled for mis-quotes a few feet above the pond. A feeling of being connected overwhelmed Corey. He wasn't someone viewing the pond; he was part of the pond. He knew it. The pond knew it. The pilot from yesterday was clueless.

In the stillness of the morning, Corey saw a dark form slide into the water. With the heightened senses that a small amount of adrenaline brought, he studied the ripples it was making. Logic took over. Logic was good. Logic made sense. Logic was the opposite of emotions and he'd had enough emotions to last a lifetime. His first thought was that the shadow had been that of a mammal. No, too small for an otter, too little wake for a muskrat. When the animal surfaced for a second time, it was close enough for Corey to make out the head of a turtle, but he could not lock in on the exact species. Probably an eastern painted turtle. Maybe, if he was lucky, it was a Blanding's turtle and he could take credit for finding an endangered species. The only way to know for sure was to wait it out and hope it would get close enough to make a positive identification. The turtle dove again. "It made a slow descent, so it may not have seen me," Corey deduced.

The pond surface turned to glass. Corey treaded water just enough to stay afloat. As time passed, he started to put some pieces together. It was early July, a time when adult female turtles set out looking for sandy places to bury their eggs, usually on a well-drained, south facing slope. Something about this didn't fit. Painted turtles liked to bask on a log or a rock. There were no good basking sites here. Painted turtles are small, usually less than ten inches in diameter. This was larger—much larger. Logic. "What are the chances of its being a Blanding's?" Corey thought, "That would be a good thing, and good things don't happen to me—at least not any more."

The large snapping turtle surfaced just three feet from Corey's head. Logic was gone and fear took over. Both animals were using the same primitive part of their brain. A cerebrum was of no advantage at this point. One animal screamed. The other would have if it could. Swimming faster than he had thought possible, Corey quickly reached the shallow water. His feet hit the muck and he started running. He didn't worry about not liking muck.

Looking back at the water, he could see only the bubbles and the muddy cloud that this encounter had created. Out of breath and shaking slightly, Corey got dressed. This was the second time in two days that his swimming had been interrupted. But today was different. The pilot was clueless as to what an ecosystem was all about. The snapping turtle was part of it. Corey was mad at the pilot. He respected the turtle.

Much calmer now, Corey smiled and started the long walk home. He had to admit that it had been exciting, not that he would want to do it again. Back in town, his classmates were probably getting their kicks sitting in front of a computer screen. His classmates were stupid.

It was 10:55 when Corey reached the farmhouse. He filled a glass of water and sat down at the kitchen table. Ellen gave him a strange look when he reached over and turned up the volume on the radio.

"Good morning. I'm Alice Gerardi," said the voice, sounding like a woman who'd never seen a real prairie, or skinny-dipped with a snapping turtle. "Joining me today is Dr. Bill Whitehorse from the University of Wisconsin Extension Office. He is a botanist, a Native American, and the author of the book, *Restoring the Grasslands of Wisconsin.* He's here with us to talk about the role of wildflowers in a grassland ecosystem."

Corey was hanging on every word.

"Before we take our first call, I'd like to ask our guest an important question. What is the historic significance of wildflowers in poetry?" Openly disappointed, Corey turned the radio off and left the room.

20
The Letter

"Hey, Corey, there's a letter here addressed to 'Cor Nelson.' Any idea who that would be?" Ben walked into the kitchen carrying the mail.

Corey's eyes opened wide even before the smile hit his face. "That's got to be from Uncle Jeff. He's the only one who calls me 'Cor.'" Corey sat down at the kitchen table and eagerly ripped open the envelope.

> Cor,
>
> It's been a while since I've had a chance to talk to you. I haven't seen you for so long. I'll bet you're growing like a weed. I suppose I should tell you that Judy and I have split up and I am staying at a friend's house. She wants a divorce, but I'm still working on a way to get her to change her mind.
>
> I hope you are happy with your decision to leave and that your foster parents are treating you well. Please let me know how you are doing. Remember, families stick together.
>
> Uncle Jeff

Ben noticed that the boy's enthusiasm had lessened a little by the time he finished the letter. "So, how's your Uncle Jeff doing?" Ben asked.

"Okay, I guess. He may be getting a divorce, but maybe not."

"That's too bad. I hope things work out for him."

"Yeah, well—Uncle Jeff is not real good at making things work." Corey said quietly.

"How so?" Ben asked, adding, "If it's none of my business, I'll understand."

"No, that's okay. It's just that he does some dumb stuff sometimes. He drinks a lot. He even had his driver's license taken away once. He can't keep a job and then he gets real mad at everyone. I know that he and Judy have been fighting a lot. I think it has something to do with not being able to have kids." As if to take the harshness off his words, he added, "Uncle Jeff can be a ton of fun sometimes too."

Corey reread the letter and then said, "There's one part I don't understand."

"What's that?"

"He said he hopes I'm happy with my decision to leave. I didn't decide to leave—he kicked me out. He just walked into the living room, started calling me…well, he started using bad words, and then told me to 'pack my things.' I was gone that afternoon."

"And in our house two days later," Ben thought to himself. He was torn. On the one hand, he knew the boy had been hurt badly by his uncle. On the other, if Jeff hadn't thrown him out, Corey would not be living with them. Ben placed his hand on the back of Corey's neck and said, "Well, I think things worked out pretty well."

Corey tipped his head straight back, in a way that had him seeing Ben upside down. "Me too."

Ben didn't say how good those two words made him feel. Instead he suggested, "It might be a good idea to write your uncle back. I'm sure he would love to hear from you."

"Cool!," he said as he walked up to his room.

Watching Corey leave, Ben said, too quietly for anyone to hear, "Andy would have loved having you as a little brother."

Corey sat at his desk in his room and tore a sheet of lined paper from his English notebook.

Uncle Jeff,

It was nice to hear from you. I'm sorry to hear about you and Judy. Things are going okay here. Ben and Ellen are real nice, but I do miss Mom and Dad a lot. Some days I think about them so much, it's hard to think of anything else.

They are treeting me reel good here. The food is good (except the meat loaf) and sometimes we go on trips to neet places. I had a teacher in school that was giving me trouble. You should have seen the way Ellen stood up for me. That guy didn't know what hit him when she was done.

They have a dog named Poncho. He's fun to play with. Now that the weather is warm, I spend most of my free time at the Barrens. It's a wildlife area just down the road. It's the type of place that Mom and Dad would have loved.

I have to go and do my chores so I'll have to end. Thanks for writing. Please write again.

Cor

21
Bill

The half-inch goldenrod spider clung motionlessly just below the unopened bud of the coreopsis. Its white abdomen had, what looked to Corey like pink lightning bolts on its side. Judging by its size, it was likely a female. If he waited long enough, Corey was sure he'd be able to watch her feed. Lying on his stomach in the grass, he was set to wait for hours. He didn't need to wait long. A woolly bear caterpillar moth flew past, circled around, and landed on the top of the bud. Corey watched intently as the spider, making almost imperceptible movements, crept closer and closer to its intended prey. As the spider rounded the curve of the bud, the moth began to show signs of nervousness. The spider moved close enough to strike. Corey watched without breathing.

"Hey, what are you doing down there kid?" a loud voice shouted from only a few feet away. Corey jumped, twisted, and gasped all at the same time. In a panic, he quickly tried to identify the large man standing over him. Still on the ground, he began to move away while not taking his eyes off the stranger who had just set a large pack on the ground.

"Who are you?" Corey asked angrily.

"I'm sorry. I didn't mean to scare you," the stranger said. "It just took me by surprise seeing you here."

"Who are you and what are you doing here?" Corey asked again.

"Look, I'm really sorry I scared you," said the man picking up his pack and taking a step backwards. "I'll come back some other time to finish my work." Before he turned to walk away he added, "My name is Bill. Bill Whitehorse."

"You're that guy who wrote the prairie book, aren't you?"

Now it was Bill's turn to be surprised. "How in the world does a little kid know something like that?"

Corey stood up and brushed the dead grass off his clothes. "I'm not a little kid and I know more than you think."

"Let me ask you the same question then," Bill said. "Who are you?"

Corey stepped forward and extended his hand. "I'm Corey Nelson. I'm staying just down the road." Bill Whitehorse shook his hand, held it for a longer time than would have been expected, and smiled.

This made Corey nervous. "What's wrong?" he asked, unsure of how to read Bill's reaction.

"I don't know why I didn't see it right away."

"See what?"

"You look so much like Tom it's amazing."

"You knew my dad?"

"I worked with your dad for a few years in Madison. We shared an office. He was a great guy and a hell of a botanist. I knew your mother, too. I'm really sorry."

A chill passed through Corey. In the five months since he'd left Madison, Bill was the first person he'd met who'd actually known his parents.

"I was in Kenya when I got the news. There was no way I could have made it back for the funeral."

"The only person my dad ever talked about in Kenya was some guy named Stogie."

Bill pulled a cigar out of his pocket and said, "That's me, 'Stogie' a.k.a. Bill Whitehorse. When we were working on our doctorates, I had the bad habit of smoking cigars to stay awake. Once your father even locked me out of the office until I promised not to light up. We did have some fun together. Then I went on to Ohio State to take a teaching position. If it weren't for e-mail, we would have lost track of each other long ago. I just moved back to Madison a month ago to start this new job." Bill put the unlit cigar back into his pocket and asked, "How old are you, Corey?"

"I'm thirteen."

"You would have been about three years old when I left Madison."

"I've grown a little since then."

"I'd say. So, what's a thirteen-year-old kid doing in a place like this?"

"I like it here. There are all kinds of cool plants and the birds are great. I almost got to see a goldenrod spider have lunch, but someone interrupted me."

Dr. Whitehorse knelt down to examine the spider, still sitting on the flower bud. Turning to Corey, he said, "I really am sorry about that."

"What are you doing here?" Corey asked.

"This is one of ten prairie sites I'm studying across the state. You would have known that if you'd read the book."

"I've never seen the book. I just heard about it."

"The plan is simple. I'll be visiting each site about once a week from now until the snow flies, taking field notes on the animal activity I see. I'll also be collecting seeds from the prairie plants and replanting them nearby to start a

112

new prairie."

"Prairie restoration—cool! But ten sites?"

"I said the plan was simple, not easy."

"What's in the pack?" Corey asked.

"Just basic field supplies; a laptop, a cellular phone, and a GPS unit."

"What's a GPS unit?"

"It stands for Global Positioning System. It uses satellites to tell us exactly where we are."

"Sounds pretty high tech to me."

"I have a pencil and a pad of paper too."

For the next hour, the two naturalists talked about the things they had in common; prairies and Tom Nelson. As they walked along a deer trail that twisted its way through the Barrens, Bill was impressed by everything Corey knew. It was clear that, by nature or nurture, Corey was very much like his father.

They made their way back to Bill's car as it got close to three o'clock. Corey was expected home to do chores and Bill was expected at his daughter's softball game back in Madison. As Corey got on his bike, Bill reached into the back seat of his car. "Here," Bill said, handing Corey a copy of his book. "You can read it if you need help falling asleep."

"Thanks!"

"If nothing else, at least read the first page."

Corey rode home one-handed. He couldn't wait to tell Ben and Ellen about Bill Whitehorse.

At first Ellen was a little concerned about Corey meeting a stranger who said he knew him. After he showed her the book, she relaxed. "If you run into him again, ask him to stay for dinner. We'd love to meet him."

Later that evening, Corey sat in bed with the book, beginning with the first page...

This book is dedicated to my wife and daughter, who taught me the meaning of joy, and to my good friend Tom Nelson, who worked to save the natural world he loved for the son he loved even more.

Corey closed the book while fighting back tears. He suddenly found himself missing his parents more than he had in a long time. He quickly got dressed and went downstairs. Ellen was sitting on the sofa watching TV as Corey sat down next to her. She put her arm around him without saying a word.

Four days later just before nine in the morning, Ellen heard a knock on the kitchen door. As she opened it, a tall man with a backpack said, "Hi, My name in Bill Whitehorse. Is Corey home?"

"Oh, hello there. Corey told us about you. Come on in. Can I offer you a cup of coffee?"

"Sure, sounds great."

"Corey's in the barn. He should be back in a minute."

"Actually, I'd like to talk to you first." Bill Whitehorse had just finished explaining the reason for his visit when Corey walked in. The two naturalists greeted each other.

"I thought I recognized your car. What's up?"

"Well, I've got a problem I'd like you to help me with. It turns out that you were right—ten sites are a lot of work. I'm looking to hire some talented people to help me out."

"I'm in!" Corey shouted.

"Not so fast, Sunshine!" Ellen said.

"What I need is to find someone who can identify prairie plants, collect seeds, and take decent field notes. Do you know anyone who fits that description?"

"There's one name that comes to mind."

"The job pays five dollars an hour for eight hours of work each week. I'll expect you to mail me your field notes once each week, along with a sample of the seeds. So, do you want the job?"

Corey looked at Ellen, knowing that the decision was not entirely his.

"It's okay with me, as long as you don't go overboard with it."

"Way cool!"

Bill and Corey went over some details about how to collect seeds and complete the field notes. Bill offered Corey a laptop to take his field notes with, but he immediately turned the offer down. "Computers and I just don't get along," he said.

"If you change your mind, let me know."

Bill drove away and Corey planned to start his work immediately.

"Hold on," Ellen said. "I want you to finish cutting the lawn and weeding the beans before you even think about heading to the Barrens." Corey reluctantly left to complete his chores.

By one o'clock in the afternoon, Corey was walking through the Barrens with a field bag and a notebook. He had to admit that things had definitely improved since school was out. Ben and Ellen were great. He still missed his parents, but the really bad nights didn't come as often. Bill Whitehorse treated him like a real botanist, and Steve and Wendy would be back in just a few days.

114

Corey sat down in the tall grass and just let the world go by. The wind felt great as it blew through his hair. He saw a wood tick climbing on his jeans. He picked it off and held it in his hand, close enough to see all eight legs. His dad had explained that they always like to climb up, so he pointed his finger upwards. Sure enough, it climbed to the top of his finger. He pointed his finger to the ground and it changed directions and headed toward his wrist. The predictability of the tick was refreshing. Not too many things in Corey's life had been predictable. "How would it climb in zero gravity?" he wondered. "When I become a graduate student, I'll design an experiment to check it out." He flicked the tick into the grass and made a note to be sure to check his clothing for other ticks before he got home.

A baby thirteen-lined ground squirrel, looking like skinny chipmunk, popped its head through the grass and looked at Corey. More curious than afraid, it stood on its hind legs and stared at him. Corey laughed and it ran away. Tree swallows dived at Corey's head and scolded him as he walked deeper into the Barrens. "The bird houses set out by some Boy Scout troop must be full of eggs," Corey thought. In the distance, a northern harrier hawk worked the field looking for mice and the sandhill cranes were showing their chicks how to catch bugs.

With a notebook full of information, Corey took a quick swim in the duck pond and headed home to fill out his report. It was an incredible day. High above him, an eagle flew lazy circles. Corey saw it but told himself he hadn't.

Wisconsin Prairie Remnant Inventory
Field Notes

Location: *Mary G. Lincoln Wildlife Area*

Date: *July 2*

Weather conditions: *Sunny, 85 degrees, light winds*

Researcher: *Corey Nelson*

Plants in Bloom: *spotted knapweed , black-eyed Susan, monarda*

Seed Collected: *lupine, prairie smoke, spiderwort*

Wildlife:

tree swallows, northern harrier

thirteen-lined ground squirrel, bluebirds

sandhill cranes , wood ticks

Narrative: *Bill, I hope this is what you're looking for. The bluebirds were working on their nest. The swallows were atacking my head! The crane chicks are about the size of big footballs and they are yellow-brown.*

I notised alot of spotted knapweed along the roadsides in this area. How come it isn't a problem here in the Barrens?

Thanks again for letting me do this.

Corey

July 5

Hi Corey,

Your field report was exactly what I was looking for. You will need to work on your spelling. Also, baby cranes are called colts.

As far as spotted knapweed goes, here's my short lecture. It was first planted in gardens because the purple flower was pretty and it was easy to grow. Now it has invaded millions of acres of grassland all over the United States. Knapweed will thrive on any disturbed soil; that's why it's found along the roadsides and doesn't grow in the middle of the Barrens. Wildlife can't eat it and it has reduced the carrying capacity of grassland by up to 90 percent in some areas. Some studies show that knapweed gives off chemicals which kill the surrounding vegetation. The plants' many seeds can stay dormant in the soil for years, so even if you kill the knapweed you see, more will be back next year.

Keep up the good work. Say hello to Ben and Ellen for me. I'll be by to see how you're doing in a few weeks.

Bill

22
Ellen

Ellen heard the slam of the screen door and the barking of Ponch outside, as Corey hopped on his bike for a summer morning of adventure in the Barrens. Inside, these familiar sounds brought back memories that had been painstakingly kept at bay.

The only thing Andy had loved more than his bike was the ball of black and white fur Ben had brought home for his twelfth birthday. At first, Ellen had not been pleased. She had never been a dog person and didn't like the thought of a shedding animal in her house. This was one of the few times Ben had made a major decision unilaterally. It took only a few days to see that Andy and Ponch would be inseparable friends.

Andy's love of trains had started almost from birth. The electric train set in the basement had been the focal point for hundreds of hours of father/son time. Every Sunday in fall they dragged the old black and white TV into the basement so they could watch the Packer game while running the train set. It didn't matter that the train caused such bad interference on the small set that it was difficult to watch the game. Their halftime entertainment was always the same. Andy had several small football helmets that the local gas station was giving away. The Green Bay Packer helmet had been just the right size to fit over the front of the train engine. The Chicago Bears' helmet took its place on the track in front of the oncoming train. When the inevitable crash occurred, the shouting reached the living room. "It must be halftime," Ellen would say to the empty room.

There wasn't a sport Andy hadn't excelled at, and his proud parents never missed a game. At times, work on the farm would extend late into the night because Ben had spent the earlier hours cheering on his son. Although Ellen complained about standing in the cold rain to watch football games, the truth was that she loved every minute of it. Small sacrifices were a part of parenting.

In school, Andy had blown hot and cold. Any class that had required him to have two feet on the ground at the same time was destined to be troublesome.

Viola Williams, the energetic science teacher had gotten Andy through seventh grade science by making sure he'd always had assignments written down and by creating projects that Andy found interesting. She had also been the first to suggest that he might have a reading problem. After some testing and some modifications in how he studied, his grades had begun to improve. It had still been a battle to get him to read. His eighth grade English teacher believed in letting her students select which novels they would read, and that had helped. He'd always picked a novel that had some connection to farming or sports. A milestone was reached the day Andy had come down from his bedroom thrilled because he had actually read a whole book.

Any spare time had been spent working with Ben in the barn. Andy enjoyed farm work and had talked about someday being a farmer—or a football player—or a high school wrestling coach or...

The ringing of the telephone shook Ellen from her memories. It was Karen Conley asking Ellen to serve on a committee to look into building a new library. It had been eight years since Ellen had done any committee work. While Andy was in school, Ellen had been the ultimate in school moms. Her involvement was so welcomed, and so well-known, that teachers had openly cheered when they saw Andy's name on their class list in the fall. She'd done it all; chaperoned field trips, run fund-raisers, served snacks at parent meetings, and even organized the teacher appreciation day.

But that was when Andy was in school. Andy was gone, and so was her enthusiasm for being around other people. Ben had to take over the grocery shopping. For several years she stopped going to church, so she wouldn't have to see people she knew. Her withdrawal from life had continued until she would not even leave the house or answer the telephone. With their marriage in trouble, Ben had finally gone to Reverend Olsen for help. His regular visits had helped Ben and Ellen to rebuild their relationship and make plans for the future.

They had reluctantly agreed to think about being foster parents—Ellen wasn't sure she could do it. In the middle of a March blizzard, Reverend Olsen had driven all the way out to the farm, saying, "this isn't something I can explain over the phone." Reading the file he'd brought about a small boy who had lost his parents, was all Ellen or Ben needed. Their discussion had taken place completely through eye contact. Knowing the risks involved in saying yes and the certainties involved in saying no, Ellen had turned to Reverend Olsen and said, "We'll do it." The next evening Corey was in their house and their lives had begun again.

"Sure, Karen, I'd love to help with the library committee. Just let me know when and where."

Wisconsin Prairie Remnant Inventory
Field Notes

Location: *Mary G. Lincoln Wildlife Area*

Date: *July 9*

Weather conditions: *Sunny, 78 degrees, calm winds*

Researcher: *Corey Nelson*

Plants in Bloom: *leadplant, purple prairie clover, thimbleweed, black-eyed Susan*

Seed Collected: *needlegrass*

Wildlife:

hummingbird, kestrel

Narrative: *Bill, it rained most of the week, but it was clear today. I collected some needlegrass seed although it looks like most of it needs another week or so.*
  I've noticed that people are dumping trash along the roads near the Barrens. Last week I found two tires and a refrigerator.
  Corey

  P.S. I had Ellen check my spelling.

July 11

Corey,

I've been in meetings for four days. It sounds like you're having more fun than I am. Get this, they want me to be on public radio again in September. Brush up on your wildflower poetry because if I have to do it, you're coming with me. Who knows, maybe we can actually get her to talk about prairie plants!

The trash you're seeing is an unfortunate result of new laws that were meant to protect the environment. People have to pay a small disposal fee when they bring tires and refrigerators to a land fill, so some people try to save money by just dumping them along some remote roadside. If you see anyone doing that, try to get a license plate number. For now, give your town chairman a call and tell him what you found.

Thanks again,

Bill

23

The Complaint

Now that summer was here, Corey could stay out in the Barrens until 8:00. Ben and Ellen were both sitting at the kitchen table when he got home. He knew immediately there was a problem.

Before he could say a word, Ellen said, "Corey, could you sit down. We need to talk with you."

Something about the tone of her voice struck fear in the young boy. "Sure, what's up?"

"We got a call from Cindy Dalea tonight."

Corey didn't know if he heard anger in her voice, or concern. "She's the lady from Social Services that brought me here."

"Yes. It seems that your Uncle Jeff has filed a complaint against us. He says we have been treating you poorly."

"The exact words he used were physical and emotional abuse," Ben added. Corey looked confused.

Ellen continued, "You have always been honest with us, so whatever you tell us, we'll believe." She paused to think about how to ask the next question. "Did you tell your Uncle that you didn't want to be here?"

"No!" Corey said, "I told him about you guys and Ponch. I told him about how I like to go to the Barrens and all of the trips you take me on."

"Did you tell him you were unhappy here?" Ben asked.

"I told him that I miss my parents—that I miss them a lot."

Ellen sat forward on her chair and said, "Think Corey, and this is important, was there anything else you said to make him think you were unhappy?"

Corey hesitated and then admitted, "I told him I don't like your meat loaf."

Ben laughed and said, "Neither do I!" It was clear that Jeff was wrong, or had just misinterpreted Corey's letter. The confusion and hurt that Corey was feeling showed in his eyes.

"Thanks Corey," Ben said. "We'll phone Ms. Dalea in the morning and tell her that it was all a big mix-up. Don't worry about it."

Corey did worry about it, but he kept it hidden. He explained that he was bushed and went up to bed. Sleep didn't come easily and when it did, it didn't last long. Shortly after midnight he was knocking on Ben and Ellen's bedroom door.

"Come on in, Corey," Ben said sleepily. Corey came in and sat down on the edge of the bed. "What's up, Buddy?"

Corey said slowly, as if he had practiced, "I just want to be sure that you know that I didn't...I mean...after everything you've done for me...I wouldn't tell anyone I wasn't happy here."

Ellen sat up and put her arm around him. "Look, you told us what happened and we believe you. Now would you please go back to bed and try to sleep." Before letting him go she gave him a long hug.

As Corey started to get up he looked at both Ellen and Ben and said quietly, "I love you."

"We've known that for quite a while," Ellen said. "We love you too, and I promise we'll still love you in the morning if you let us get some sleep." Corey smiled just a little and left.

The next morning, Ben called Cindy Dalea and explained what Corey had said.

"That's pretty much what I figured, but we've got to look into these things anyway," Cindy said.

"Well at least it's over," Ben replied.

"It's not quite over," Cindy said. "We'll have to do a complete investigation and after that, I'm sure it will just die in a file somewhere."

"What type of investigation?" Ben asked.

"Routine stuff. Corey will need to see a doctor and talk to a child psychologist."

"Is that really necessary?"

"Just between you and me, no. But we'll get in a heap of trouble if we cut corners. I'll set up the appointments and then call you with the details. Tell Corey not to worry about it."

"That's easy for you to say."

"I know it's a hassle, but it's important that we don't give anyone any reason to get excited. In the meantime, I'll ask around about Jeff Nelson."

"I still don't understand why you or Ben can't take me," Corey said on the day of his appointments.

"Ms. Dalea said that she would take you. That way no one could say that we were coaching you."

"Are they going to take me away from you?" Corey's question was so direct it took Ellen off guard. She couldn't tell him that she was wondering the same thing.

"No. Now be good." She hugged him and he walked out the door. Corey noticed that she had been hugging him more often lately, but he didn't mind.

The first stop for Cindy Dalea's Chevy Suburban was at the office of Dr. Gordon Carex. Corey studied the sick people in the waiting room while Ms. Dalea read a magazine. An elderly man had a bad cough and a young boy had a broken leg. Corey felt sad as he listened to a woman try to explain to the receptionist that her young daughter was sick but she didn't have any money. He could see that she loved her daughter and wondered why the little girl's father wasn't there to help.

"Corey Nelson," a woman with a clipboard called.

"I'll wait here," Ms. Dalea said. Corey was relieved. He was shown into a small examining room that smelled like rubbing alcohol. Ten minutes later, Dr. Carex came in.

"Hello there, who do we have here?" He looked at the chart.

"I'm Corey Nelson."

"It says here that you're staying with the Raines."

"Yes, sir."

"Well, you are a very lucky young man. I've known them for a long time."

"Then you knew Andy?"

"Yes. I was Andy's doctor. He was a great kid." The doctor closed his clipboard. "Well, here's the plan. We're going to do some lab work, I'll need to do an examination, and then we're done."

"Let's get it over with."

Corey walked out of Dr. Carex's office forty five minutes later. The next stop was at the office of Dr. Jacob and Associates. Corey was shown into the office of Lisa Mephitis. "She must be one of the 'Associates,'" Corey thought. The office looked like someone's living room—someone who didn't have kids. Corey's next thought was, "I'll bet she listens to public radio."

Ms. Mephitis took out a small tape recorder and pressed record. She also opened a black notebook and began to write. "Well," she said without looking up, "I'm glad we could get this chance to talk. Why don't you start by telling me a little bit about yourself." That was the last of the easy questions. For the next two hours, Corey answered question after question, each seeming to be a little more personal than the one before. He found himself saying things aloud that, until that time, had been only private thoughts. With each answer, Corey looked at the tape recorder and wondered who would be hearing this. By the time it was all over, Corey had learned to hate recorders, personal questions, and Ms. Mephitis.

Ellen was waiting impatiently at the door when Cindy's car pulled up. Corey ran into the house as Cindy waved good-bye and drove away. Ellen busied herself as he came in.

"I know you're going to ask, so why don't you sit down and I'll tell you all about it. Unless you want me to wait until Ben gets home."

"He won't be home until late; it's your call," Ellen said as she sat down at the table.

"Let's talk now. If I don't tell someone, I'll pop."

"If you don't tell me, I'll pop."

"Well, we went to Dr. Carex's office first. He said all kinds of nice stuff about you and Ben."

"He was Andy's doctor."

"He told me that."

"How did the rest of the visit go?"

"It was okay, I guess. I was a little uncomfortable with parts of it, but not too bad. They needed a blood and urine sample. I hated the needle, but I didn't flinch. Then he checked me all over. That was a little embarrassing. He asked me about how I got every little bump and scratch he saw. He also asked about some guy stuff. Most of the time he talked about the Minnesota Twins. Dr. Carex must know everything there is about baseball.

"Talking with Ms. Mephitis was the worst. You said I had to answer every question truthfully, and I did, but she asked some really personal questions. She kept asking about the things I think about and stuff—things I've never had to talk about to anyone. She had a tape recorder going the whole time. She can't let anyone hear that tape can she?"

"I'm sure she's a professional. Look, don't worry about it. Everyone has times when they get embarrassed."

"Even you?"

"Oh yeah! Once, when I was in the sixth grade, I was standing in the top row of the chorus singing in a Christmas concert. Everybody was dressed in their Sunday best and the place was packed with parents. I had the flu but I talked my mother into letting me go anyway. To make a long story short, I threw up and wiped out fifteen kids."

Corey laughed. The story seemed to take the edge off the day.

When Ben got home Corey was in bed. Seeing light coming from under the door, he knocked.

"Come on in."

"Hey Bud, I hear it was a little rough today." Ben sat down on the bed.

"Yeah."

"Feel like telling me about it?"

"Didn't Ellen explain it all?"

"I'd like to hear it from you."

Corey sat up a little in his bed. "Dr. Carex was okay, I guess. He thinks you're cool, but..."

"But you still had to get undressed and let him poke around in places that you would rather not have poked?"

"Yeah, how did you know?"

"Been there, done that!"

"It's not that I'm shy about that stuff—you see me in the pool locker room almost every week, but..."

"I know what you mean."

"Ms. Mephitis was the worst. Do you remember the time that you and I sat up and talked all night?"

"Sure."

"That's the stuff she kept asking me about. But it was like she didn't believe me. She was asking me if I had done stuff I had never even heard of. I tried to tell her that I didn't know what she was talking about and she started to get mad at me."

"Were you honest?"

"Yes."

"As honest as you were with me?"

"Yes."

"Then you have nothing to worry about."

"What if someone hears that tape?"

"Then they'll find out that you're a perfectly normal thirteen- year-old boy. Now, what was it she was asking you that you didn't understand?"

"Have you got a few hours?"

"If that's what it takes." A half-hour later, Ben turned out Corey's light and stood up. "I love you Buddy."

"I love you too," Corey said, adding, "That's on her tape too, and I don't care who hears it."

Wisconsin Prairie Remnant Inventory
Field Notes

Location: _Mary G. Lincoln Wildlife Area_

Date: _July 16_

Weather conditions: _cumulus clouds, 101 degrees, light winds_

Researcher: _Corey Nelson_

Plants in Bloom: _butterflyweed, coreopsis, monarda, leadplant_

Seed Collected: _needlegrass, blue-eyed grass_

Wildlife:
_bald eagle, brown thrasher,
deer with two fawns, little frogs everywhere,
the crane colts have grown a little larger_

Narrative: _Bill, There have been a lot of jet fighters flying low over the Barrens. Are they ever loud! Also, isn't it strange to be seeing eagles this far away from water?_

A major storm came through in the afternoon. Some buildings south of here were damaged. (Have I ever told you I hate storms?)

This was not a good week at home. I'll tell you all about it the next time you're up here.

Corey

July 18

Corey,

Another great report. Thank you. I would have thought you'd love storms. I'm sorry things aren't going well at home. I'll be up in a day or two so you can tell me about it then.

If you look at a map, you can see that the Wisconsin River is not that far from you, so seeing eagles every now and then isn't really out of place. I've heard of a pair of eagles nesting somewhere in the backwaters near you. If I find out the exact location I'll let you know.

I also made some phone calls about the jet fighters. It seems the Air Force has started another round of training runs at the bombing range near Babcock. Please call my cell phone number if you see that the flights are upsetting any of the critters in the Barrens. I'm particularly concerned about the cranes. As far as I know, no study has shown a problem from low-level flights, but I'd like you to keep an eye on it anyway.

Take care,

Bill

24
Talking With Bill

"I feel like I should be in a parade," Corey said as he carried the Global Positioning System antenna. The eight-foot pole had a round disk on the top and was connected by a shielded cable to the GPS receiver that Corey wore around his neck.

"That's an awfully expensive baton you're carrying," Bill said.

"I don't see why we need all this stuff. Can't we just write it down on paper like I do in my field notes?"

"Your field notes are fine, but this is different."

"I don't get it."

"Okay, one more time. The GPS uses the satellites to pinpoint our exact position. We feed that data into my laptop and from there I'll use the cellular modem to e-mail it to the computer on my desk back in Madison. That information, along with the work we do the rest of the summer, will become an overlay in a large geographic information system, or GIS, for short. When combined with digitized base maps of this area, we can generate maps of exactly where the prairie remnants are. That's just the start. If we can get the bugs worked out of the system, we can take the show on the road—literally. Think about it: school kids could help locate prairie remnants in their area, e-mail the data to us, and BINGO, we have ourselves a map of all of the prairie remnants in the state."

"If you think that schools would be interested in something that cool, I'll introduce you to Mr. Culex. If he can't teach it with a worksheet, it won't happen."

"You have to look at the big picture. Those remnants are sitting right under peoples' noses and they're the key to the restoration projects."

"Will there be a restoration in the Barrens?"

"It's hard to say. The first precaution of intelligent tinkering…"

"Yeah…I know, 'To keep every cog and wheel…'" Corey looked out at the clouds on the horizon.

"Why do I get the feeling that your mind is somewhere else today?"

"Sorry. It's just that there's a bunch of stuff going on at home."

"I'm a good listener."

"My uncle told Social Services that Ben and Ellen were not being good foster parents, but it's not true. They're real nice to me, maybe more than I deserve. I asked Ellen if I was going to be sent away but she said 'no.' I think she's just trying to keep me from worrying about it."

"What makes you think you'll be sent somewhere else?"

"I don't know. Ever since this thing with Jeff, Ellen seems to be real nervous. She's always hugging me when I come home."

"Sounds like she's just glad to have you around."

"They've also been going to meetings at Social Services, but they always change the subject when I ask about them."

"Could it be that you're just making too much of this?"

"Maybe." Corey stooped to look at a lupine growing along the trail. "Can we talk about something else for a while?"

"Sure. Pick a topic."

"Tell me what it's like to be an Indian...I mean, Native American."

Bill laughed. "Where did that come from?"

"I've never known a real Native American before so I was hoping you could answer some questions for me."

"I'm not sure what I can tell you, but fire away."

"Okay, for starters, why don't you have long hair?"

"I don't have long hair because I choose not to have long hair." There was just a hint of unpleasantness in his voice. "Let me save you some time. I don't live in a tepee, I don't sleep on the ground, and I couldn't shoot an arrow ten feet."

"I'm sorry. I didn't mean to get you upset."

"I know, it was a fair question. I guess I overreact sometimes. But let me put it this way, you told me once that you resented it when the kids at school made judgments about you before they knew who you were. The way many people think about Native Americans is similar. They have bad information, or no information at all, and then they think they know everything about anyone who is an Indian."

"Can I ask you about your religion?"

"Sure, I'm Roman Catholic. What do you want to know?"

Corey looked disappointed.

"Why do I get the feeling that's not what you wanted to hear?"

"I read that Native Americans have sacred places and I was hoping to learn more about them. Sorry."

"Don't be sorry. There are many Native Americans who feel a special link-

132

age to the land. Some have certain places they go to when they need to get reconnected. In some cases these places have been used for centuries. To be honest, I don't know too much about that."

"Do you have a place you hold sacred?"

"For me, It would be the Highground Veterans Memorial Park, outside of Neillsville. That's west of Marshfield," Bill added. "My sister was killed in Vietnam. When I'm in that area, I like to stop and look out at the landscape and remember all the good times we had. Every time I go there I can't help but think how she would have loved the view from the top of that hill. Once again, this was not what you wanted to hear."

"No, that's okay."

"I think you need to talk with my grandfather."

Wisconsin Prairie Remnant Inventory
Field Notes

Location: _Mary G. Lincoln Wildlife Area_

Date: _July 23_

Weather conditions: _Sunny, 82 degrees, windy_

Researcher: _Corey Nelson_

Plants in Bloom: _butterflyweed, red milkweed, monarda, black-eyed Susan, spotted knapweed!!!_

Seed Collected: _spiderwort_

Wildlife:

grasshoppers, prairie chickens,
eastern bluebirds, savannah sparrow, hognosed snake,
badger (holes only, but they must be badgers)

Narrative: _Bill, Thanks for talking with me. It helped a lot._
I saw prairie chickens! This was the first time I saw them
this summer. They flew up as I was walking through some
brush. The crane colts are growing fast and are turning
darker. They still can't fly but they can walk real fast.
Grasshollers and butterflies are all over the place!

Corey

25
A Short Note From Jeff

Ben and Ellen tried not to look anxious as Corey sat at the kitchen table opening the letter from Jeff that had just arrived. Corey had insisted they be there when he opened it. Slowly, as if expecting bad news, he tore the paper flap away. A single folded page was inside. "I really hate notes," he thought to himself. He unfolded the letter and began to read the almost illegible printing,

> Cor,
>
> By now you know that I tried to get you out of that awful home they put you in. My request for custody was turned down, but please don't worry, I'll keep trying. For now, just don't do anything stupid. It would help our plan if you would send me specific details of how badly they are treating you.
>
> My divorce will be final in September, but I think I can get Judy to change her mind before then. Think of it, all three of us together. You'll be part of a family again, I promise.
>
> Uncle Jeff

Shaken, Corey handed the letter to Ben. After reading it silently, he handed it to Ellen, who inhaled deeply when she finished reading it. "He's confused, don't pay any attention to this letter," Ellen said, doing a poor job of hiding her concern.

"Why didn't you tell me that he'd asked for custody?"

"We didn't want to worry you," Ellen said.

"Besides, Social Services feels this is the best place for you," Ben added.

"For now," Corey said. "What about the next time?"

"Look, they did a background check on your uncle and found a few things he didn't tell you about," Ellen said.

"Like what?"

"They wouldn't say. But it was enough to keep any judge in the country from giving Jeff Nelson custody of anything."

"Are you telling me the truth this time?"

Ellen was at first taken aback by the tone of the question, but quickly realized that it was probably justified. "We should have told you, but we didn't want to worry you. I'm sorry." Ellen put her arms around Corey and held him.

"Do you think I should write him back?"

"No! I think that would be the worst thing you could do," Ellen said.

"But shouldn't I tell him that I really want to stay here?"

"I think he already knows that," Ben said.

Corey sat in his bed with a tablet of paper. Ben and Ellen were wrong. If he could just explain how good things were and how much he wanted to stay here, Jeff would be happy. Jeff was family and family did what was best for each other. What was best for him was to stay with the Raines. Jeff loved him and would understand.

> Jeff,
>
> Please stop saying that I am not happy here. This is the best place I've been since Mom and Dad died. Ben and Ellen love me and I love them. I want to stay here forever. When you say the things you did in your letter, I get scared. If you care about me, you'll understand.
>
> Maybe someday you can come and visit us. I could show you how nice it is here and then you would know that I am being cared for very well. I'd even take you to the Barrens. That's my favorite place to be. Every day I ride my bike there for a few hours in the morning and again after lunch.
>
> Please, let me stay here. I think it's what Mom and Dad would have wanted.
>
> Love, Cor

Next morning, Corey slipped the letter into the mailbox after Ben put some bills in so he wouldn't have to explain why the red flag on the mailbox was up. He rode off to the Barrens to collect seeds.

Off in the distance a flock of high-flying geese formed a "V." Corey's heart sank. "It's too early!" he thought. "It's mid-July!" To Corey, the geese meant only one thing—summer would soon be over and school would have to start again. School was stupid.

Wisconsin Prairie Remnant Inventory
Field Notes

Location: *Mary G. Lincoln Wildlife Area*

Date: *July 30*

Weather conditions: *Overcast, 74 degrees, light rain*

Researcher: *Corey Nelson*

Plants in Bloom: *blazing star, yellow coneflower, monarda, western sunflower, butterflyweed, spotted knapweed*

Seed Collected: *leadplant, black-eyed Susan, yellow coneflower*

Wildlife:

whitetail deer, turkey, striped skunk

Narrative: *Bill, More butterflies! I've seen more monarchs this week than I have all summer. With all the rain we've had, it looks like it could be a good year for big bluestem. Things are going okay at home—could be better.*

Corey

August 3

Hi Corey,

Got your last two reports, nice work. I've asked my grandfather to join us next Thursday in the Barrens. We'll meet you by the wooden sign around 1:00. I have to recheck the numbers the GPS is giving me. That will give the two of you a chance to talk.

See you Thursday,
Bill

26
Meeting Grandfather

"Corey Nelson, I'd like you to meet my grandfather, Anthony Whitehorse." The three of them were standing at the entrance to the Barrens.

"It's nice to meet you, young man. Bill has told me all about you."

"It's nice to meet you too, sir."

"Please, call me Tony."

Corey studied Tony's face. His wrinkled skin and shoulder-length hair, with streaks of gray, fit more closely the picture Corey had of what a Native American looked like. A silver bolo in the shape of a bear paw hung in the middle of his denim shirt completing the picture.

"I'm going to head back to the car to fix the GPS. That will give you and Grandpa a chance to talk." With that, Bill left.

Corey shifted his weight from foot to foot, not knowing what to say. "Should we sit on the ground?" Corey asked.

"You watch entirely too much TV—besides, I'd get my pants dirty. Let's just go for a walk. Bill says you know a great deal about this place, so how about giving me the grand tour."

"Sure." Corey began to feel more comfortable. Talking about the Barrens was something he could do at anytime and with anyone.

Fifteen minutes into the walk, Tony changed the subject. "Bill said you had something important to ask me."

"I do, but I don't know how to say it."

"Words are always a good way to start."

"Okay, but if it's too stupid, just tell me."

"Out with it!"

"What I wanted to know about was the connection that Native Americans have—or maybe had—with the land." Corey waited for mocking laughter, but it didn't come.

"That's a rather perceptive question for someone so young."

"It's just that I've been reading about how cultures around the world seem to have places that are sacred—or spiritual—I'm sure I'm not using the right words here, but…"

"You're trying to figure out why this place has become such a part of you."

"How did you know?"

"I told you before, Bill filled me in on your background. I can also tell by the way you talk about it. It's the same way my neighbor talks about his Jeep."

Corey laughed.

"The best I can do for you is to tell you what I know."

"That would be great."

"First of all, it would be misleading to talk about Native American culture as if it were a single thing. It would be like saying that all of Europe was the same. I have some friends in France who would not take too kindly to being lumped together with the British. But I think we can get away with making a few generalizations." A deer mouse dashed across the trail as they walked.

"The land has been the source of food, water, and beauty for as long as people have been on earth. Our cultural practices reflect the importance of that fact. Plants that were used to treat illnesses came from the earth, as did the clay for pots and the reeds for baskets. When we die, we're buried and our bodies become part of the land again. So I guess that it only makes sense that there is a reverence for the land.

"Unfortunately, many people today, including some Native Americans, have lost touch with the land. They spend too much time in air-conditioned buildings and eat in fast-food restaurants. The only connection to nature they have is by watching wildlife documentaries on public TV. When they do get outdoors, it's often on a noisy snowmobile or those little jet boats. I know that doesn't answer your question…"

"It helps," Corey said. "Thanks."

"Go ahead and ask that other question."

"How did you know?"

"I can see it in your face. By the way, you'd never make a good poker player."

Corey paused to think about how to phrase his question. "Have you ever had an animal talk to you…I mean in real words?"

Tony looked surprised for a moment. "No, not really." An awkward moment of silence passed and then Tony continued, "Tell me a little more about this."

"Maybe I'm just going nuts, but something really strange happened last March. Have you ever seen the eagles feed along the river in winter?"

"Yeah, it's incredible!"

"Ben and Ellen took me there when they found out I like birds."

"That was nice of them."

"Yeah, it was great."

"But..?"

"Well, I had this eagle land right in front of me…maybe."

"What do you mean maybe?"

Corey looked to the sky, almost expecting to see a large bird soaring overhead. "I think it may have just been a dream, but I wasn't asleep…and it talked to me."

"Like what?"

"It was almost as if my parents were telling me that I was going to be all right."

"Maybe they were."

"What?"

"Look, I'm no shaman, and frankly I don't understand much about that sort of thing, but I believe we all carry a part of the loved ones we've lost with us. I believe that their love—their memories—continue to guide us as we go on with our lives. In that way, we are never really alone."

Corey did a double take when he heard those last three words. There was no way that logic was going to convince him it was only a coincidence.

Tony continued, "Sometimes when I'm walking on my farm, I think about my granddaughter, Bill's sister. I can't say that I actually hear her voice, but it's as if, in a way, she's there with me. Especially in the spring when the apples are in bloom. She loved my apple trees. Now, anytime I smell apple blossoms, I think of her."

"For me it's hearing cranes," Corey admitted.

"I wish I could be more help, but what fun would life be if someone told you all the answers?"

"You mean if someone handed you the cheat codes?"

"I don't get it."

"It's a long story."

"Here's my advice, and it's got to be good, because I'm an old fart."

Corey laughed.

"Don't believe everything you read, keep looking for the answers to tough questions, and keep listening to the voices you hear."

"Thanks."

As they walked back toward Bill's car, Tony added, "You're a good kid, Corey. If you're ever passing through the reservation, stop in. I'll tell Bill to bring you up for a weekend sometime."

"Cool. Do you have an Indian sweat lodge?"

"No, but I have a Finnish sauna." Tony smiled and added, "Yet another stereotype crashes to the ground!"

27
Jeff Makes His Move

Corey pedaled into the gravel driveway after a successful morning of work in the Barrens. He hadn't collected any seed, but he did find a small stand of compass plant. This would be exciting news to tell Bill, and Corey couldn't wait to mail in his field notes. He even considered calling him to tell him the good news. Rosa, the sixty-eight-year-old mail carrier, pulled her car up to the mailbox. Corey admired how well she could drive from the passenger side of the car. She steered with her left hand and controlled the brakes and gas with her left foot. She put a large collection of envelopes into the box and drove off.

Corey put the bike in the barn and walked out to the road to bring in the mail. With a rusty squeak, the mailbox door opened and he grabbed the handful of bills and catalogs. Sorting through the stack on his way to the house, he found the letter from Jeff. At first he didn't even want to touch it, almost as if it were radioactive. Sure that Ellen would be upset if she saw it, he stuffed it in his shirt.

Corey dropped the mail on the table, yelled "Hello," and went upstairs.

"Hey Corey, I'm heading to town to do some shopping. I'd like you to come with me," Ellen called from the living room.

"Okay," he called back. Corey stashed the letter under his pillow and headed down to join Ellen on her shopping trip.

"There's a back-to-school sale going on. I thought we could get an early start at getting you some school clothes."

Ordinarily, talk of school starting again would have ruined Corey's day, but he was thinking too much about the letter. So he made no protest as they stopped at three stores and he tried on at least ten pairs of jeans. They arrived home just as Ben was returning from work.

"I've got a great idea. Let's go out for pizza," Ben said.

"Good idea," Ellen said eagerly. "We've been gone all day and I don't have a thing ready yet." They went inside just long enough to drop off the packages and get cleaned up. The letter would have to wait until later that evening when he went to bed.

Lying in bed, Corey looked at the sealed envelope. Maybe, he thought, he should just throw it out. Maybe he should tell Ben—he'd know what to do. Corey took a deep breath and opened the envelope.

> Cor,
>
> Your long wait is over. By the time you read this, I'll be on my way to pick you up. Don't worry about your foster parents, if they try to stop us, they'll be sorry. I don't want to hurt anyone, but after what they've done to you, it would serve them right. Pack your things and wait for me. When you see me pull into the driveway, run to the car.
>
> Too many people have been telling the Nelsons how to live their lives. Now it's time for you and me to show the world that we can't be pushed around anymore.
>
> Uncle Jeff

Corey had never known such fear. He was paralyzed by the thought of Uncle Jeff coming to the house. Ben and Ellen would never let Jeff take him and they would likely get hurt—or worse. There was no way he could let them suffer, he'd caused them far too much pain the way it was. Corey struggled to listen to logic, but all he heard was, "RUN!"

Corey thought back to the short time he had been living with Jeff. He could not stop thinking about the one violent outburst he witnessed. Jeff smashed a chair, threw a beer bottle against the wall, and kicked a small aquarium. As water flowed over the freshly broken glass, Jeff turned to Judy and threatened to hit her. She ran from the house screaming.

Corey tried again to use logic, but emotions won out, "If you love them—RUN!" He had no way of knowing when Jeff would come—maybe he was on his way this very minute. Hours had already passed since the mail had been delivered. Maybe Corey could think more clearly once he got away. He had no idea where he would go, but he knew he couldn't stay here.

With minutes passing like hours, Corey waited until Ben and Ellen went to bed, and then waited a half-hour after that. He stuffed some clothes into his backpack, made his bed, and slipped out the kitchen door. Ponch was at his side before the screen door quietly closed. "Please don't bark," he whispered to his good friend.

The barn door was open just enough for him to get his bike out. The darkness of the farmyard made seeing potholes difficult. By the time he was on the main road, his eyes adjusted to the darkness and the light from the gibbous moon made riding a little easier. He pedaled as fast as he could in the limited light, almost hitting a doe that was standing in the middle of the road.

He reached the large wooden sign for the Barrens faster than he had ever done before. Stepping off his bike, he said aloud, "Now what am I going to do?" Reality began to set in. He had left the farmhouse for the last time. He would never see Ben or Ellen again—it was the only way to keep them safe. He looked at the bike. It wouldn't be right to take it with him. He'd leave it here so they could find it.

He was in such a rush to get out of the house that he hadn't thought to leave a note. He pulled his field notebook and a pencil out of his pack and began to write.

> Dear Ben and Ellen,
>
> By now you know that I've left. I hope you understand that I had no choice. Jeff said he was coming to get me and he would hurt you if you tried to stop him. I couldn't let that happen. You have been the best thing to happen to me in a long time and I will love you forever. Please don't worry about me, I'll be O.K.
> Love,
> Corey

Corey wedged the note between the brake cable and the handle bar, propped the bike up carefully against the sign, and walked off into the darkness of the Barrens. He would spend the night there and then decide where to go in the morning. Maybe he would head north to find Tony Whitehorse.

Thirty minutes later, Corey was sitting on the outer edge of his favorite stand of oaks. From here he could look out over the Barrens at night. It was a sight he had never seen before. The closest he had come was the night, last spring, when he'd sat in the prairie chicken blind with Wendy and Steve. The Milky Way was stretching from horizon to horizon and the frogs were calling in the distance. Fireflies were flashing in the field and bats were doing acrobatics over his head. Corey missed all this. His mind was busy thinking about what he had just done. A wave of doubt hit him. Should he have told Ben and Ellen? Should he have called the police? Too late for second-guessing now; he was here and he couldn't go back. He settled in under an oak and waited until sunrise.

Ellen ran out of Corey's room. "Ben!" she shouted. Ben came running from the bathroom with shaving cream still on half his face. "Corey's not here and it looks like he hasn't been here all night!"

"I'll look outside," Ben said. "Maybe he decided to camp in the yard." He headed back downstairs, but before he got out the door, Ellen shouted again.

"Ben, call the sheriff!" She flew down the stairs with Jeff's crumpled up letter in her hand and tears running down her face.

As the sun started to light up the darkness, Corey realized that he had fallen asleep. He also realized that he would now have to figure out his next move. Cold and hungry, he stood to stretch. Stepping out from the trees, he heard a voice.

"Hey, Cor, I was wondering how long you were going to sleep."

"Uncle Jeff, what are you doing here?"

"You know why I'm here. It was a smart move to slip out at night. If you hadn't propped your bike up, I'd have never found you. Let's get going."

"I'm not going with you."

"Corey, I'm in no mood for this kind of childish behavior. Grab your bag and let's get out of here."

"I'm not going anywhere with you!" Corey began to shake uncontrollably.

Jeff slapped him across the face and then grabbed him by the arm. "Look, you're coming with me if I have to drag you out of here." Corey broke free from Jeff's grip and ran down the deer trail that led back into the woods. Jeff followed closely behind, screaming obscenities as he went. Not seeing the broken tree limb laying across the trail, Corey tripped and fell. Within seconds, Jeff was standing above him, out of breath. "You stupid kid, what have they done to you? They've turn you against your own family!"

"You're wrong, Uncle Jeff," Corey said through his tears. "They love me. You were the one who threw me out. You were the one who turned against his family." Corey could see that Jeff was getting angrier, but he didn't care any more. He'd had enough. "I can't help it that your life fell apart. You made some stupid decisions and now you're blaming everyone else."

As Corey got up to walk away, he saw Jeff's eyes widen and the large branch he was swinging. The jagged branch plunged into Corey's stomach, just above the navel, knocking him to the ground. The forked end of the branch acted like the talon of a large bird, ripping a seven-inch gash deep into his abdomen as he fell. Corey struggled to stand as his mind slowly processed what had just happened. He felt no pain. He simply looked with disbelief from the reddening trench in his belly to his uncle's emotionless face. Jeff and Corey stared at each other. As blood poured from his wound, the young boy felt his body grow weak while his eyes asked the question his mouth could no longer form, "Why?" Corey collapsed to the ground.

Holding his bleeding nephew, Jeff began to sob, "You stupid kid. If you'd have just listened to me. Can't you see I needed you to get Judy back? She never forgave me for kicking you out—you were the child we couldn't have. All I wanted was to have a family. Was that too much to ask?" Jeff left the dying boy in the small stand of trees and walked away.

The sheriff's deputy pulled into the yard with his lights flashing. Ellen was at the car door before he got out. "Our foster child is missing," she said. "His uncle may have tried to take him."

"Is that Jeff Nelson?"

"How did you know?"

"Iowa County just sent us a fax on him an hour ago. Seems he beat up his estranged wife and they figured he was heading up this way."

"His bike is gone!" Ben shouted as he ran from the barn. "I'll bet he's in the Barrens somewhere."

"Unless Jeff has him," Ellen added ominously.

"We'll get some people here and start a search. The best thing you can do is to stay here and wait," the deputy said to Ellen.

"There's no way I'm sitting around here while that boy is out there somewhere!"

Wendy and Steve pulled into the driveway. Steve jumped out and ran over to where Ben and Ellen were talking to the deputy. "We were listening for our birds when we saw the squad car come screaming past. Is everyone all right?"

"Corey's gone. His uncle may have grabbed him," Ben said.

"We drove past his bike a half hour ago," Wendy said running up to join the others.

"Where did you see it?" The deputy asked.

"Where it always is, by the big sign," Steve said. "We thought it was a little strange because you guys would never let him out there this early and he treats that bike like it was made of gold, so we knew he wouldn't have forgotten it."

Another squad car pulled into the driveway. The deputy talked to the officer briefly, and then the car drove away. "He's going to look around in the Barrens. Maybe he can find something."

"Unless he knows his way around, he's not going to find much," Wendy said. "It's a huge place and nobody knows it better than Corey."

"Standing around here isn't going to help. Let's get over there and find the boy," Ben said, trying to hide his fear.

By the time everyone arrived at the sign, eight local dairy farmers, crammed into two rusty pickup trucks, joined the squad cars. In a farming community news travels fast, and people don't ask if you need help—they just show up.

Steve closed up his cellular phone as he walked over to Ben. "I called Spider. He's going to get his crew in the air as fast as he can." Ten minutes later, three yellow crop dusters were buzzing the Barrens at tree top level.

Ellen walked over to the bicycle, found the Corey's note, and began to cry. Ben held her tightly. This scene was all too familiar. Losing a child once is more than most people ever experience. Enduring the loss a second time would be unimaginably devastating.

A deputy walked quickly over to them and said, "We caught Jeff. They've got him in the back of a squad car and are questioning him."

"Did he have Corey?" Ellen asked. "Is he all right?" The deputy's hesitation terrified Ellen even more. "What aren't you telling us?"

"He didn't have the boy...but he was covered with blood." Ellen closed her eyes and inhaled deeply. "I think you two should go home. We have more than enough help here."

The squad car carrying Jeff Nelson stopped in the middle of the dusty road near where they were standing.

As a volcanic rage built inside of him, Ben walked over to the open driver-side window. "What have you done with my foster child?"

Over the shoulder of the deputy driving the car, Jeff's monstrous voice rang out, "So you're the jerk who ruined my life! I guess it's too bad about that obnoxious kid. You should have let him come with me when you had the chance. Now it too late. The funny thing is, I'm the one they'll blame for his death!"

"Get him out of here," shouted Ben as the man's words sunk in. Ellen ran over to her husband. The look on his face told her all she needed to know— she had lost her second son. She put her arms around Ben and held him.

"Steve! Get over here FAST!" Wendy shouted from the Blazer, parked behind a state patrol car. Steve came running, with Ben and Ellen following quickly behind. "It's number four! Corey's trying to tell us where he is."

Steve jumped into the Blazer, threw on the headphones, and began turning the huge antenna sticking out of the roof. "I got the first heading, 135 degrees. Corey is alive and is somewhere in that direction," Steve said, pointing to the southeast.

"How far?" a deputy asked.

"Can't tell from just one reading. We need at least one more, two more would be better."

"Got no time for three—get me that second one, and fast. From the looks of Jeff's shirt, that kid has lost a lot of blood."

The deputy radioed the first heading to Spider as Steve started the car, still wearing the headphones. Wide-eyed and pale-faced, Steve shut the car off and stepped out. "You'd better pray that Spider and the boys find him, because we just lost the signal." Ben and Ellen had been doing nothing but praying.

The three small planes converged on the area from where the last signal had come. Over and over, they flew the heading two miles out and returned. The planes were so close to the ground they had to go into steep climbs to avoid hitting trees.

"We got him!" shouted a deputy as he stepped from his car. "Spider found him in some trees. There's no way to tell what kind of shape he's in, but we found him."

"What are we waiting for? Let's go get him," Ellen said.

"You'll never get back there. It's too rough. The hospital in Marshfield had a chopper returning empty—they should be here any minute." As if on cue, the faint, low-pitched drone of the helicopter could be heard. The brightly painted ambulance quickly set down in the open field next to where Corey lay.

After what was the longest five minutes of their lives, Ben and Ellen heard the news they needed to hear. "He's alive. He's in rough shape, but he's alive."

"He's just been moved to the ICU," the doctor said as she walked into the waiting room. "He's a tough little kid and he's kind of weak, but he's been asking to see you."

Two silent prayers of thanks were said as the Raines hurried to the ICU.

Pale and groggy, Corey tried to speak. "I'm sorry."

Ellen touched her hand to his lips and said, "Don't try to talk, there will be time for that later—by the way, you're grounded."

Corey smiled and said in a weak voice, "Looks like you finally get to see me wearing pajamas."

Ellen laughed.

Corey tried to raise his hand to touch her, but didn't have the strength.

"How ya doing, Bud?" Ben asked.

Corey looked up at him, struggled a smile, and fell asleep. "Maybe we should come back later."

As they walked out of the ICU and into the hallway, Ben turned to Ellen and said, "Okay, make a list for me."

"Of what?" Ellen asked.

"Of all the things you'll need from home."

"How'd you know I wasn't leaving here without him?"

"I figure the kid will be lucky if you let him go on his honeymoon without you."

"No chance of that."

The next morning, Corey was transferred to a room on the pediatrics ward. Balloons were everywhere. Ellen had asked that people wait a few days before they stopped in to see him. She made one important exception.

"Corey, I'd like you to meet Spider. He's the pilot who found you. He saved your life."

"Hello, and thank you," Corey said, his voice stronger. "What type of pilot are you?"

"I'm a crop duster. I spray the fields near your house. You'd be amazed at what I can see from up there." Spider laughed.

Corey turned red. Ellen was confused.

28
The Judge

Cindy Dalea walked out of Corey's room after dropping off yet another bouquet of balloons. Ellen followed her out. "He's looking pretty good, considering what he's been through," Cindy said.

"He'll be out in a few days and we can get our lives back to normal."

"Not yet," Cindy replied cautiously. "It seems that after Corey's story hit the wire services, relatives started crawling out of the woodwork. An aunt from Nashville has filed for custody, and I have two other calls to return on this case when I get back to the office." She observed Ellen's pained sigh. "Look, you know where I stand on all of this. As far as I'm concerned, the only place for Corey is with you and Ben. But I can't say how much weight my report will have."

"Is there anything we can do?"

"Well, you can make your case to the juvenile court judge. You have an appointment with him at nine on Tuesday. Corey meets with him on Wednesday at five in the afternoon."

The day after Ben and Ellen had their appointment, it was Corey's turn to talk to the judge. Ellen didn't say much about their appointment, only that they'd had a "nice talk."

Corey was sure that the aunt from Nashville would be taking him away. He had given passing thought to running away again but knew that that would hurt Ellen even more. It seemed that everything he did ended up hurting the people he loved the most.

Cindy Dalea drove Corey to the judge's summerhouse on the Wisconsin River. Silently he took note of how the vegetation changed as they got closer to the river. He almost said something about it to Cindy but didn't. He had decided that he didn't like her any more. He also hated the judge, even though he'd never met him. The two of them seemed to be working to take him away from Ben and Ellen and that made them the enemy.

"Hello Corey, come on in," Judge Corvin Hester said.

Corey walked into the living room and sat down on the sofa. "Has anyone told you why you're here?"

"Are you going to take me away from Ben and Ellen?" Corey asked, sounding anxious.

The judge was surprised by the boy's directness. "No decisions have been made yet. Although I don't always like it, my job is to make tough decisions and it looks like I'll have to make another one soon."

"Why can't I just stay with the Raines?"

The judge didn't respond.

Mrs. Hester walked into the room with three glasses of lemonade on a tray. She was in her sixties and had gray-blonde hair. "Would you like something to drink?" she asked.

"Yes ma'am. Thank you."

"I hope you don't mind, but I wanted Iris to meet you." The judge's voice became quieter. "I'll let you in on a little secret. In the last thirty years I haven't made a major decision without her."

Corey smiled.

"Now, you and I need to talk. I was thinking we could go for a boat ride and then come back for a cookout. Can you handle that?"

"Yes sir."

"Well you won't get any dinner if I stay in here," Mrs. Hester said. "Corey it was a pleasure meeting you."

"Thank you. It was nice to meet you too."

"Let's go take a tour of the river. There's something I'd like to show you," the judge said.

Corey followed the judge down to the river. The sixteen-foot fishing boat had a forty horsepower engine. "Can you swim?"

"Yeah, Ben and I swim every week."

"Here, just keep this near you." The judge tossed Corey a life jacket. The engine started quickly and was quieter than Corey had expected. Heading downstream, with the strong wind to their backs, the ride was smooth and dry.

"Tell me about Ben and Ellen," the judge asked.

Corey began talking and didn't stop for twenty minutes. The judge was impressed with Corey's loyalty to his foster parents. "You've given me a much better idea of what's going on than I got by looking through your file."

152

"My file?" Corey suddenly got nervous.

"Yes, your case worker sent over a ton of stuff."

"Did you read the whole file?" Corey couldn't hide the fear on his face.

"If you're asking if I listened to the tape, the answer is yes."

Corey wanted to jump out of the boat, or at least hide under the seat.

The judge sensed his uneasiness and added, "Hey, don't worry about anything on that tape. I was impressed by the way you handled yourself. Now, Ms. Mephitis on the other hand..."

"I really didn't like her."

"I don't blame you. She was a little rough on you."

"I'll say!"

"Let's just hope that Ms. Mephitis doesn't ever have the misfortune of showing up in my courtroom. I don't take too kindly to any adult who puts a kid through what she did to you."

"Can you destroy the tape?"

"Sorry. That I can't do."

"I figured."

"But I might accidentally misplace it."

Corey's face lit up just a little. "I'm old and I'm mean. If I say I lost it, who's going to ask any questions?"

Corey laughed. If it weren't for the fact that the judge was going to take him away from Ben and Ellen, Corey could almost learn to like this guy.

As they rounded a bend, the judge shut the motor off. The boat continued to drift. "You love Ben and Ellen, don't you?"

Without any hesitation, Corey said, "Yes."

"I thought so." The judge pointed to a tall white pine and said, "This is what I wanted to show you."

"Wow." Sitting in the uppermost branches of the pine was a nest almost half the size of the boat. Just above the nest a bald eagle was perched on a bare branch. A second eagle landed on the nest with something in its talons. Three small heads popped up over the edge of the nest and began begging for food.

Corey and the judge watched for a few minutes and then headed back. Once they were out of sight of the nest, the judge turned the throttle up and the small boat raced back upstream and into the wind. Corey hung on to the railing and twice checked to see exactly where his life jacket was. Cold spray hit him in the face and blew his hair back.

"Okay, so I drive a little too fast sometimes," the judge said as they pulled up to the dock.

After a simple dinner, the judge and his wife sat and talked with Corey for over an hour. At times Corey wondered why they were talking about the things they did. Sports, music, and the need to understand algebra had nothing to do

153

with where he would be living. The judge drove him home. Along the way, they talked even more. "You're an awfully impressive young man," the judge said as he pulled into the Raines' driveway. "Iris thinks your terrific and she's never wrong about anyone."

"Are you going to send me away?" It was clearly the only thing on his mind.

"Corey, you'll just have to trust me."

On the morning of the hearing that would decide where Corey would be living, Ellen knew for sure that three people had not gotten any sleep. In truth, the count was closer to fifteen people, most of whom showed up in the Adams County Juvenile Court to show their support. Looking around, Corey saw a sea of familiar faces. Reverend Olsen, Wendy and Steve, Bill and Tony Whitehorse, Spider, Karen Conley, and Principal Danaus were all sitting in the back of the courtroom. The door opened one more time and Don walked in. He flashed Corey his trademark dopey grin and sat down in the back.

Corey sat with Ben, Ellen, and Cindy Dalea at a table on one side of the room. On the other side sat a lawyer and Grace Mustela, an aunt that Corey had never met. She was the one who had filed for custody. The judge walked in and sat down.

"Ladies and gentlemen, my name is Judge Corvin Hester. I'd like to welcome you to my courtroom. I'll say that once more for emphasis, this is MY courtroom and in MY courtroom things run MY way. Any questions so far? Good." There was an attitude of cocky self-confidence in his voice. The judge got out of his chair and walked to the middle of the room. "This is not a trial. No laws have been broken here. We are here simply to find the best place for this young man to live. Let me say from the start that this sounds like a good problem to have. In a world where people are homeless, we have several people arguing that they should be given the privilege of acting as the guardian of Corey Nelson.

Normally, we would put people on the stand, ask a bunch of questions, and I would leave to make my decision. However, this young man has been through far too much for things to be normal. He will not need to take the stand; in fact, no one will."

The lawyer for Grace Mustela started to stand and the judge cut him off. "Don't even think about saying a word." The look on his face melted the lawyer back into his seat. "I've already met with all the parties involved. I've talked with Mrs. Mustela and the Raines." I had a very nice evening with Corey. The truth is, if I were twenty years younger, Iris and I would have

154

adopted him on the spot. My summaries of those meetings are on file; anyone is free to read them if they feel I've made a mistake. Unfortunately, the records from the office of Dr. Jacob and Associates have been misplaced. If they show up, they will also be available." Corey smiled. "After careful study I have decided that it would be in the best interests of this child to remain in the temporary foster care of Bill and Ellen Raine."

Ellen grabbed Corey so fast that it hurt his stomach wound. Ben wrapped his arms around both of them. The cheers from the crowd drowned out the vulgarities that Mrs. Mustela used with her lawyer. In truth, she wasn't here because she wanted Corey, but because she was family and felt obliged to clean up the mess that Jeff had created.

"Ben and Ellen, I'd like you to stay for a few minutes," the judge said, as the crowd of exuberant people stood to leave. Corey noticed that the judge didn't seem happy. Others sensed this also, and the crowd of supporters quickly calmed and sat down. The judge continued. "For starters, I'd like to tell you, Corey, that you are truly a remarkable child. I was serious when I said I would adopt you if I were twenty years younger. Iris and I both feel we have been blessed to get to know you and hope that you will visit us often."

"Thank you, I will," Corey said softly, feeling uncomfortable.

"Now, Ben and Ellen, I suppose I should be commending you for what you've done for Corey. You took him into your home and made him a part of your family. But unfortunately, I know what's been happening in that house and, damn it, it's going to stop right here and now." The anger in his voice seemed to be building. "Do you love that boy?"

"Yes," Ben said, looking both fearful and confused.

"Speak up, I can't hear you!"

"Yes, of course we love him."

"Then why on earth haven't you fought to adopt him?"

"We filed a request to adopt him, but they told us that foster parents wouldn't be considered. It's their policy."

Corey turned and looked wide-eyed at Ellen. He had no idea they had even tried to adopt him.

"We didn't want to give you any false hope," she said to Corey.

The judge continued in anger. "This is exactly what I'm talking about. You tell me that you love this child and yet you let some low-level bureaucrat stop you from adopting him."

"But..."

"Just keep quiet, I'm not done yet. I have two legal documents sitting in front of me and one of the two of them will get my signature this morning. Which one I sign is up to you." He held up a piece of paper. "This one is a bench warrant for your arrest, for all of the senseless stress you put this child through." The judge held up the second document. "These are the adoption papers that would give you permanent custody of Corey Nelson."

Ben and Ellen were stunned. Corey stopped breathing for a moment.

"Make a decision folks, do you want a son, or do you want to go to jail?" Ellen reached over and grabbed Corey. Ben pulled the boy away from her and wrapped his arms around him tightly.

In a much softer tone the judge said, "Hold on, it's not that easy." Ben loosened his grip on Corey and turned to the judge. "I have not heard either one of you ask Corey if he wanted to be adopted." The judge paused and added, "and you had better make it good, because I've worked pretty hard to get you folks to this point."

With a gentle assist from Ben, Corey stood to face the two people who were about to become his parents. The room fell silent. Through eyes that were filling with tears, he watched as Ben and Ellen struggled for the right words. Ben spoke. "Corey—you've brought two very lonely people back to life. We need you to go one step further." Ben waited, thinking about what to say.

Ellen continued for him. "What Ben is trying to ask is…will you please be our son?"

Corey didn't answer. He slowly wrapped his arms around Ellen and did not let go. Over the cheers and tears of almost everyone in the room, Corey whispered into Ellen's ear, "Will you please take me home?"

Ben and Ellen drove their son home. In a few days, they would celebrate with a large gathering of friends—but not today. Today they would take some time just for themselves, to say the things that needed to be said. Today they would simply be a family.

Without needing to look up, Corey knew that somewhere, high above him, an eagle was spinning effortless circles. The restoration was now complete.